Made in the USA
Coppell, TX
25 September 2020

THE CLOCKWORK MENACE

BEC MCMASTER

LOCHABER PRESS PTY. LTD

ISBN: 978-1-925491-07-4

❀ Created with Vellum

1

L *ondon, 1877*

MASCULINE LAUGHTER ECHOED through the hotel door, followed by a distinctly feminine giggle.

Perry Lowell grimaced as the elevation chamber doors closed behind her at the Charing Cross Hotel. She could hear a faint murmur now; words she couldn't quite make out—and was grateful not to.

She rapped her knuckles against the door. The laughter froze, a listening quality echoing through the stillness. "If it's housekeeping... then we're not at home to visitors."

Another feminine giggle followed the man's words.

"Get your backside out of bed, Garrett," she shot back. "It's Perry."

That brought about a flurry of movement inside. "Give me a moment."

"Oh, stay love. Tell them to go away, and stay with me,"

the woman cooed, as the sound of bare feet padded on the floorboards within.

"Business, I'm afraid." His smooth voice hinted at a smile and Perry could just imagine what was going on behind the door – Garrett snatching at his clothes as he winked, and made smooth promises to the friendly widow he'd been cultivating. She'd seen it all before. Women loved Garrett, and he loved women.

Perry stepped away, and peered through the window in the hallway, giving him the illusion of privacy. Or perhaps not wanting to hear those whispered love words, and promises he'd no doubt break.

Garrett had been her partner for nearly six years, after she'd arrived at the Guild of Nighthawks one night, soaked to the bone, and shivering with the dark hungers of the craving virus. Her first few months as a blue blood had been horrendous as she struggled to rein in her bloodlusts as her body slowly changed; becoming leaner, faster, stronger, and hungrier. Not for food though. Only blood.

The door jerked open and Garrett appeared, his shirt still half unbuttoned and a bite mark on his neck. Perry caught a glimpse of the plump widow who wore nothing more than the froth of sheets in the middle of the bed. An ice bucket housed an open bottle of champagne by the smell of it, and sheer, gauzy lace fluttered over an open window, beneath red, swagged drapes. The smile the woman had worn for Garrett faded as she caught sight of Perry, becoming a little sharper, a little narrower. Then the door closed, and it was just the two of them.

"I thought we had the day off?" he said, buttoning the shirt to his throat and hiding that condemning mark.

"Unfortunately, someone forgot to mention that to the criminal classes," she replied. The scent of somewhat rancid lilies wafted through her sensitive nostrils as he drew closer. Perry screwed her nose up. "You smell like a whorehouse."

"And how would you know what a whorehouse smells like, my lady peregrine?"

Touché. As one of the only two female blue bloods in London, she was expected to be above reproach, in all respects. The aristocratic Echelon who ruled the city, had decreed that only males were to be given the blood rites that infected a human with the craving virus, and began the transformation into a blue blood.

The Echelon feared that a female's sensitive nature would be unable to deny the strong lusts and fierce cravings of the virus. Perry was determined to prove them wrong. She sipped her blood in private, using her own money to purchase it from the draining factories the government collected the blood taxes at, and maintained herself with a fierce decorum. Indeed, Garrett often told her she was almost puritanical, which bothered her a little.

Not everyone could be as careless as he though.

"So what is urgent enough to drag me from a rather pleasant bed?" he asked, thundering down the stairs in front of her, and slipping his black leather coat - the uniform of the Nighthawks - over his broad shoulders.

"My apologies. Perhaps I should have waited another five minutes - that's how long the ladies keep your interest, isn't it?"

"They keep it for considerably longer than five minutes." The sound of affront in his voice faded with the appearance of the devilish grin he shot her over his shoulder. "But not a great deal longer, you're correct. You shouldn't sound so prudish. All work and no play, Perry... Makes a girl... dull."

That smarted. "Does a murder sound interesting enough?"

The smile died on his face, his blue eyes sobering. "Who?"

Holding onto her own frustration seemed petty too. "An actress at the Veil Theatre, possibly."

"Possibly?"

"The body hasn't been found yet, only... traces of blood, I'm told. Whatever that means."

NOW THAT TRANSPORTATION HAD IMPROVED, and the streets were safer at night, theatre had begun to face a little of a reconnaissance. Broad Street, in the middle of SoHo, had begun with the intent of being as grand as nearby Mayfair, and after a brief battle, had slowly given ground to the theatres, music halls and brothels.

They disembarked from an omnibus, near the Newcastle-upon-Tyne pub, and Garrett scanned the cobbled streets. Eating houses and pubs lined the streets, though a man could find much more than something to serve his stomach if he looked for it. The occasional window advertised 'French Lessons Given', and Garrett had seen places where they corrupted the *tableaux vivants* art form into something a little more risqué. At night, women of ill repute would stroll the streets, with their skirts edged just high enough to reveal their petticoats. He'd seen worse, growing up in the East End, though he preferred not to think about his past. Still, he usually felt more than a little pity when he saw the hard-etched desperation on the women's faces, and the tight, false smiles they displayed. There was nothing he could do about it, of course... But he never forgot that his mother had worn a smile like that, toward the end.

"Have you ever been to a play?" he asked Perry, in order to shake off the grim thoughts plaguing him.

She looked as solemn and sober as always, her short, dyed black hair pomaded into neat, glossy strands. It often hung over her gray eyes, as if she were hiding from the world, but wearing it swept back like that gave a sharp slant to her cheekbones, and the firm set of her chin. A stubborn chin. It matched her well. Only Perry could frustrate him enough to make him want to bang his head against the wall.

They'd been partners for nearly six years, and he still sometimes felt as though he barely knew her. She was good at what she did; she could track a criminal from the barest scrap of scent, and she was devilishly clever. Some of the men ribbed him for having to work with a female, but none of them knew what Garrett did.

He'd volunteered.

Having her as a Nighthawk went against all of the rules, and had set the Guild on its ear. She might be a blue blood, but she was a woman. As far as half the lads went, it should have been the end of the story. If the Echelon had gotten wind of it... Well, they'd come down harshly on rogue blue bloods like himself - those that had been infected by chance, not selection - and Garrett didn't care to think of what they'd do to a woman. Force her into an asylum perhaps? Someone had to keep an eye out for her, and he knew he was the best choice.

Glancing at the playbill, she hesitated. "I'm not a complete bore. I have seen several plays, a long time ago. It's difficult now that I'm a Nighthawk. I rarely know when I'm going to get a day off."

This was interesting. He knew next to nothing about her life before the Nighthawks, but there was no point asking for more. She'd only clam up. "I've heard of this one," he replied, instead. "'*A Season for Scheming*'. Mrs. Scott claimed it's terribly wicked and witty."

"Is this Mrs. Scott of the rumpled bed sheets this afternoon?"

"Yes." Though he could think of a dozen other ways he could refer to the widow. Mrs. Scott of the very ample cleavage. Or Mrs. Scott of the very clever tongue. Garrett smiled to himself. Her prejudices were showing. "One would think you raised in a nunnery."

"My favourite play was *Phèdre*." There was a wistful note to her voice that he nearly missed.

Good God, did the sphinx just reveal something about herself? They were forced to part around a pair of ladder-men, with their cans of paste, ladder, and posters advertizing Tucson's Luxury Soap, then came back together. "A tragedy?"

"Not everything has to be a comedy, Garrett."

"Life is meant to be laughed at. How else can you keep smiling in this kind of world?"

She looked startled, then thoughtful.

"I'm not trying to be philosophical. You and I both know the reality of the London streets. There's nothing better than a good comedy, or a night out with the lads, to clear those kind of memories, and make it easier to forget the day's case."

"I read," she admitted. "It takes my mind off the worst cases."

They both felt silent. With the ruling class of blue bloods deeding humans few rights, there was little he hadn't seen, in the course of his investigations; bodies drained of blood and discarded in the gutter like so much refuse, or young girls kidnapped off the streets and sold into slavery... It made a man weary in a way that could threaten to drown a soul.

"Here, we are." He paused in front of the Veil Theatre. The poster advertised, *'Murder. Mayhem... And mistaken identity.'* "Well, we've got two out of three," he said, pushing open the door and ushering her inside.

The moment they entered the Veil, a small crowd of people hastened to meet them. Two of the women looked visibly distraught, whilst the man in front swallowed hard before coming forward to meet them with an outstretched hand.

"Nighthawks Reed and Lowell." Garrett flashed his identity card at them.

"Thank goodness," the man replied. "I'm Mr. Fotherham, the director. This is my wife, Mrs. Fotherham, and Miss Radcliffe, our lead understudy. She's the one who found... well, found Miss Tate to be missing."

Garrett tugged out his pocketbook and flipped to a blank page. "Missing? I thought the telegram said murder?"

They all shared a glance, then hurried to speak in a mangle of voices. He managed to work out the logistics. Miss Nelly Tate was the actress playing the lead role of 'Clara' in the play, and had gone missing earlier that morning. Miss Radcliffe, her understudy, had gone to fetch her for a final rehearsal for tonight's opening, and found only a few drops of blood in her room, and her leg.

"Her leg?" Perry asked.

Miss Radcliffe hesitated. "I think I shall have to show you," she said, in hushed tones.

"And no sign of her since?" Garrett continued, with a friendly smile.

The actress' shoulders softened as she shook her head. "Nelly's always so punctual. Six hours is a notable length of time for her to be missing. She's not at her home," Miss

Radcliffe finished. "We sent one of the stagehands to check, and well, the blood, you see..."

"Any relatives we might be able to talk to?"

Miss Radcliffe bit her lip. She was the type of woman who seemed to overplay every emotion, but he wasn't entirely certain if that meant she was hiding anything, or whether she was simply overdramatic.

She was also very lovely, he noted, in an entirely masculine way that had nothing to do with the case.

"Nelly never spoke of anyone," Miss Radcliffe admitted. "Though I gained the impression that her mother never approved of her stage ambitions. I believe there might have been words said at one point, and that Nelly had nothing further to do with her parents."

"What's going on?" The loud voice cut through the quiet of the theatre. A gentleman snatched his bowler hat from his head, and strode down the aisle. From the finely waxed points of his moustache, to the elegant ruff of sable fur along his coat collar, his appearance screamed *money*.

"Lord Rommell," Mr Fotherham stepped forward. "I'm afraid there's been some terrible news."

A blue blood of the Echelon then. Garrett's gut tightened. "Lord Rommell." He stepped forward and offered his hand. The man shook it with a firm grip, his dark eyes raking over the group. "I'm Detective Garrett Reed, of the Nighthawks."

"You're somewhat underdressed, aren't you?" Rommell's gaze slid over his attire.

"I wasn't expecting to be called out today." Garrett snapped his pocketbook shut.

"Lord Rommell is one of the theatre's owners," Mr Fotherham interceded. "He often comes to peruse a rehearsal."

"What's all this about, Fotherham?" Rommell's dark brows drew together as he tugged off his shiny, black leather gloves. "I thought we were due for rehearsal? Not Nighthawks."

"It's Miss Tate, my lord," Miss Radcliffe said earnestly. "She's been missing all day, and there's blood in her room."

Rommell froze. "Nelly's missing?"

Nelly. Garrett slid a glance toward Perry, whose brow twitched faintly.

"Well, what are you standing around for?" Rommell snapped. "I thought you Nighthawks were part bloodhound. Off you go! You bring her back. She's a valuable asset to this theatre."

She *might be dead.* Garrett ground his teeth together. He was used to dealing with the Echelon lords. "I was just about to recommend such a thing," he said. "Miss Radcliffe, would you care to escort us to Nelly's dressing room? Mr. and Mrs. Fotherham, no doubt we'd like to speak with all the theatre staff shortly, if you could arrange for that?" Still smiling, he shot Rommell a look. "That includes you too, my lord."

"Me?" Rommell looked aghast.

"You want her back as soon as possible, don't you?" Garrett asked, trapping the man.

Rommell's jaw worked, his eyes darting at the assembled witnesses. "Yes, yes. Of course."

∽

"So what do you think?"

Perry watched as Garrett prowled the room.

Nelly Tate's dressing room was significantly more opulent than expected. A painted silk screen stood in the corner, with a red robe discarded over the top of it and a good half dozen slippered heels were scattered around the base of the wardrobe. A splash of blood sprayed up the screen and Garrett examined it, particularly the height and size of the spatter. His jaw locked tight - no doubt the scent of the blood was rousing the darker, more predatory part of his nature.

"Not enough blood to be deadly," he said, with a tight swallow, "but she - or someone - was certainly struck a blow, most likely to the head."

Perry caught a glimpse of herself in the enormous mirror in the corner as she circled the room, a dark blot of shadow in the cocoon of pink-wallpaper. She felt distinctly out of place here.

"For a theatre starlet, she's certainly earning more than Miss Radcliffe." Perry glanced through the items on the vanity; expensive mother-of-pearl hairbrushes, a gleaming silver clockwork-locking jewelery box with expensive pieces strewn carelessly inside, powders, brushes and a brooch that would cost six month's worth of Perry's wage. The difference between Miss Radcliffe and Nelly Tate's attire was immediate.

"It depends if all of this comes from her wage," Garrett disagreed, "or a lover. Blue blood lords frequently take an actress as a mistress, especially if she were as beautiful and witty as Miss Tate supposedly is."

"Something to enquire about," Perry noted. There was a long polished chestnut box almost hidden in the corner. "It seems strange that Miss Radcliffe made no mention of a lover." She'd talked almost non-stop about Miss Tate on the way to her rooms.

"What have you found?" Garrett followed her toward the box.

"I'm not quite certain." Perry knelt and examined the case. "It's locked."

"Allow me."

Usually he carried a lock-pick set with him, but his afternoon with Mrs. Scott had obviously left him unprepared. Perry plucked one of the pins from Miss Tate's dresser and handed it to him and he set to work.

Sometimes she wondered if Garrett had ever been on the wrong side of the law. He was very good at getting into places he wasn't supposed to, or unlocking doors that were latched.

The lid sprang open, light gleaming back off the metal inside. Perry frowned, "What in blazes?"

Garrett lifted the item out, his hands cupping beneath the smooth curve of a metal thigh and caressing the elegant calf. "It's... a mechanical leg. A woman's leg."

Of course he'd notice that. Perry knelt down, running her fingers over the creation. It seemed designed to fit within a matching metal hip socket, and the patella floated free. The work was exquisite, with all of the hydraulics and pistons hidden inside smooth steel sheeting. Quite often, the work on a mechanical limb was crude, with the spars bare to the gaze. This obviously cost someone quite a lot of money.

"No synthetic skin," Garrett noted. He rolled it over, revealing elegant brass flowers etched down the outside of the thigh, like the embroidery on a stocking.

Perry tilted the foot, noting the flex of it. The knee joint also moved in response. "I've never seen the like."

"Not unusual. Most mechs don't advertise their disability."

For good reason. Most mechs were trapped in the walled enclaves the Echelon owned, where they were forced to work off their 'mech-debt' to the government in payment for their new limbs or clockwork organs. Sometimes those debts took fifteen or twenty years to pay back.

"Do you think it belongs to Miss Tate?" If it did, then how the devil did the actress afford to pay for such a creation? The sheer artistry of the limb dictated at least a twenty-year stint in the enclaves.

"Not certain." Garrett traced his fingers over the joints, searching for the numerical stamp that would indicate which enclave and mech the limb had been registered to. "If it is Miss Tate's, then I doubt she would have mentioned it to anyone."

The ruling Echelon might have thought humans a lesser class than blue bloods, but at least humans had some rights. A mech on the other hand, was considered not completely human, with their mechanical enhancements.

"If it is Miss Tate's, then I doubt she had a blue blood lover," Perry said. "She couldn't have kept something like this secret, and he'd have been disgusted."

"There's no serial number."

"What? Every mechanical limb is required by law to be registered."

"Unless it wasn't created in the enclaves."

"But... the only other blacksmiths belong to the Echelon and they're kept under lock and key." Only the Echelons blacksmiths knew the secret to creating truly functional bio-mech limbs, where flesh combined with steel, tendons fusing to hydraulic cables as if they were one. And this limb, as fine as it was, had never been fused with flesh. The hip socket gave it away.

Garrett frowned. "The other question is: if this is Miss Tate's, then why is it here? And where is she? There doesn't appear to be another case, so we have to presume this is the only limb she owns."

"If it isn't, then I think I ought to become an actress." It certainly seemed to pay better than a Nighthawk.

"I'd like to see that," Garrett drawled. "You on stage, trying to feign emotion."

It wasn't as if she hadn't spent the past six years hiding everything. Perry snorted under her breath. If only he knew just how good an actress she truly was.

He smiled, then surveyed the room. The smile died. "No sign of a struggle, apart from the blood."

"Think they hit her from behind?"

"Perhaps. Either way it indicates someone she knows."

"How did they remove her then?" Perry glanced at the bloodied screen. "Nobody claims to have seen anything unusual."

"The whole place is a warren," Garrett replied. "I don't think I could have found my way here without Miss Radcliffe to guide us. Perhaps it's easy to slip about unseen?"

"Let's do a thorough search here then, just to be certain there's nothing we missed," she said, turning back to the vanity and the letters there. "Then we'll see what else we can find in the rest of the theatre."

THEY SPENT the next couple of hours thoroughly interviewing the actors and actresses. Garrett took the lead. He was far more comfortable with making an interrogation seem like a conversation, and he swiftly put the suspects at ease, flashing quick smiles at the ladies. Perry watched, with her arms folded over her chest and her eyelids lowered sleepily. People's expressions and the tone of their voice were often far more telling than they thought, and if they were hiding something she might be able to pick it up.

Her first instinct of Miss Radcliffe made her back bristle. The pretty young actress had a wealth of naturally curly, red-gold hair and she blinked earnestly at Garrett as he questioned her. Garrett's smiles grew a little deeper and Perry glanced away as she felt the mood of the room shift. Miss Radcliffe's anxious expression relaxed, replaced by a slightly coy smile, and when he asked her if Miss Tate had been 'seeing someone', she rested her hand on his sleeve.

The woman was beautiful. It shouldn't have mattered. She was exactly the type of waifish, pretty blonde that usually caught Garrett's attention. And it was clear it was caught. Perry shifted against the doorjamb, scowling a little as she looked away from the pair of them.

"I couldn't say," Miss Radcliffe said in response to his question. "Nelly... well, I've not realized until now, but she was the sort who always asked questions about you, rather than telling you anything about *herself*." A pretty blush stained her creamy cheeks. "Some of the other girls have... well, admirers, but not Nelly. Nor myself."

Garrett glanced up from his notebook and the faintest of smiles curled over his mouth as their eyes met.

Good grief. Perry pushed away from the door. Garrett shot her a look, and she made a circling motion with her finger, letting him know she was going to have a look around.

What did it matter if he was flirting with a witness? It wasn't the first time she'd seen him take an interest in a young, attractive woman. It certainly wouldn't be the last.

Perry prowled her way across the stage, pushing the thought from her mind. She spoke to several of the stage-hands on her way, gaining a good appreciation for Miss Tate. The results were conclusive.

'Kind-hearted.'

'Not like some of those actresses you get, who usually play the starring roles...' 'I couldn't possibly fathom who would actually want to hurt her.'

"What did Miss Tate do after hours?" she asked the man who managed the lighting. "Was she... walking out with anyone?"

"Couldn't rightly guess." His gaze slid away. "She kept to herself a lot." A frown, before he looked at her earnestly. "You don't think she's in trouble, do you?"

"Well, she did get them flowers, remember, Ned?" One of the stagehands called. "Six months ago, on her birthday." He tipped his head to Perry. "I'd almost suspect she had a beau, though she never mentioned one, but she were awful excited about the flowers. Showed 'em to everybody and they was only peonies. Considering she gets sent roses all the time from the patrons, you wouldn't think they was much, would you? Gets 'em once a month now."

Perry jotted that down. *Interesting.* No doubt theatre rumor had been all over that little titbit. "When were they delivered? After a performance?"

"Nope, during rehearsal. First time she's ever stopped a rehearsal." The man shook his head. "Wanted to get 'em straight in a vase before they wilted."

Very interesting. Perry tapped the pen against her notebook.

It looked like Miss Tate had a beau.

And, she thought, her eyes narrowing slightly, it hadn't taken Garrett's rapport with people to work it out, which was a good thing, considering his current distraction...

2

"Something bothering you?" Garrett asked, as they hopped down from the omnibus, a half-mile from Nelly's home.

Stormy gray eyes the color of thunderclouds glanced up at him, but Perry looked slightly distracted. "What?"

Garrett shifted the case with Miss Tate's leg inside it, getting a better grip on the handle, as they turned toward Nelly's house. "You seem distracted."

A long moody silence ensued. "No. Just... some things never change, do they?"

"I'm not certain what you mean."

Perry finally looked up from her boots, her strides long and loose-hipped, and her hands hiding in the pockets of her long leather coat. "I was just thinking about human nature. It rarely changes, especially on a case like this."

He had the feeling she'd deflected the answer, but he didn't push her. "So who do you like for this?"

"It's too early to tell," she replied. "There's something going on with Rommell, however. Both Miss Radcliffe and Mr. Fotherham grew distressed in slightly different ways, when you brought up his name. Perhaps it's monetary? Mr. Fotherham certainly seemed focused on the theatre's finances."

"And Miss Radcliffe?"

She took her time in answering. "My read on her is... uncertain. But I think she's hiding something. She dropped her gaze and glanced to the side when you brought up Rommell, so I think there's something there – but then that could also have been the fact that you were the one asking that question. She changed the subject fairly quickly."

He digested this. "Why would I have anything to do with it?"

Perry rolled her eyes. "Good grief, Garrett. She was practically cooing at you. Though I'd be mightily surprised if you hadn't noticed *that*."

He had noticed. His eyes narrowed. "Are you complaining about the way I ran that interview?"

"Of course not. You had her eating out of your hand."

"I'm not there to be the enemy," he said. "People respond better to a more reasonable approach. If they think I suspect them, then they tend to think they might have something to hide."

"I'm not talking about *people*."

That pissed him off and he stopped in his tracks. "You think I stepped over the line with her?"

Perry took another two steps before realizing he'd stopped. "Let's not discuss this here."

It would hardly be the done thing for two Nighthawks to be caught arguing in the streets. Who knew what the press could get their hands on? "We'll discuss it later, back at the Guild."

Just so that she knew this wasn't finished between them.

Still, the idea that she even considered his approach

today to be less than professional riled him. He never let his emotions or his flirtations get in the way of a case anymore, particularly not with a potential suspect.

He had once, a long time ago, on one of his first handful of cases. He'd let a few tears sway him away from a potential suspect, when the widow had, in fact, been a merciless poisoner. The memory still humiliated him, with the way he'd been so easily manipulated.

Christ, the Guild Master - Lynch - had nearly chewed his head off over that breach and warned him that it was *never* to happen again.

Garrett knew it was a weakness of his. He didn't like to see women cry and more than once he'd stepped between a woman and her cruel husband or pimp. Every single time he saw the blank look in his mother's sightless eyes when he'd gone searching for her that long ago morning. He hadn't saved her then and he couldn't save them all now, but sometimes he had to remember that women weren't always in need of protection. Sometimes they were just as guilty as men.

The walk to Nelly's house was silent and terse.

Nobody answered the knock. Garrett slipped the lock again and opened the door. "Hello?" he called. "Is anybody home? Miss Tate?"

The next door opened and an older woman stuck her head out. "Who are you?" Her gaze slid over their leathers. "Nighthawks, eh?"

"Indeed." Garrett smoothly introduced them both.

"I'm Mrs. Harroway, Miss Tate's neighbour. She ain't at home, if that's what you're here for."

"When did you see her last?" Perry asked.

"This morning," Mrs. Harroway replied. "When she left for the theatre, about half-nine. Why? What's wrong?"

"Miss Tate is missing," he replied, jotting down the time she'd left her home. "She vanished from the theatre just before rehearsals were due to start. We're just trying to ascertain her whereabouts."

"Oh." Mrs. Harroway clapped a hand to her mouth. "Oh, what a shame. I hope she's all right. I know it ain't quite right, what she does, but she has such wonderful manners. Wouldn't think she's an *actress*."

"Does she have many callers?"

"Not a one," Mrs. Harroway told him firmly. "I wouldn't hold much with that, and I've told her too. She said she don't like having people in her home. Says it just for her, a space away from all that madness. A private woman, Miss Tate. Don't ever see her much - nor does she say much about herself."

"Does she have family?" Perry asked.

Mrs. Harroway frowned and wiped her hands in her apron. "You know, I've ever seen anyone. As I said, she don't talk much about herself, so I really couldn't say."

"Thank you for your help." He slipped her his card. "If you remember anything - or see something unusual, could you please let us know?"

Mrs. Harroway took the card and nodded.

Garrett held the door open for Perry. The moment it was closed, he breathed in. The apartment smelled like rose petals - the kind a woman put in her drawers.

There was no sign of Nelly, not that he'd expected to find one.

An hour later, there was still no sign of anything at all about the woman herself. A mystery. Usually there were letters to be found, or a diary, or something to indicate the lifestyle of the person who lived in a home, but it were as though Nelly were only a mirage. The only hint to the woman's personality were the scattering of plays and books that seemed to litter the parlour.

"It's almost as though she doesn't exist," Perry murmured, fingering a well-worn copy of poetry. "As though her entire world can be found within these pages, but there's no hint of Nelly outside of them." She surveyed the room, as if she could see something that he couldn't. "It's almost as though this was merely a place of residence for her, not a home. It's as though Nelly hasn't found her home yet, or maybe, she's still looking for it?"

Garrett eyed her. Nelly reminded him a little of Perry. Barely anyone outside of he - and perhaps one or two others at the Guild - knew anything about her, and that was the way she preferred it.

He was starting to gain an impression of the actress. Was Nelly Tate simply another role the woman played? Did anyone know the woman beneath the polite, young actress' facade?

That thought led directly to another. Was Perry playing a role too? Aloof, taciturn young Nighthawk?

What was she hiding? And for the first time, he wasn't entirely certain if he referred to Perry or Nelly.

"Well," he said, watching Perry with curious eyes as she glanced at the back of a book. No point asking her. He'd simply watch and wonder and slowly work his way through the labyrinth that protected her. "Let's press on to the enclaves and see if there's anything in here–" He gestured to the case with the mechanical leg, "that can give us a clue about Nelly's disappearance."

After all, an unregistered mech was certainly curious.

As he fell into step behind her, he couldn't stop himself from examining the short, blackened hair that caressed her nape and wondering about that little speech.

Where's your home, Perry? For it felt, for a moment, as she'd been speaking of herself and not Nelly Tate.

THE GUARDS on the gates at the King Street enclaves let them through after a brief examination of their identity cards and they found themselves ushered into the main offices overlooking the main factory. The King Street enclaves were mainly responsible for shipping, and the enormous carcasses of half-finished dreadnoughts lined the bays. Workers crawled over them, armed with welding rigs, and sparks spat across the floors.

The overseer who met them had obviously never worked a day on the floor in his life, judging by his steam-pressed suit and immaculate tie. Garrett exchanged a glance with Perry, opening the case on the man's desk to display the leg as he introduced himself.

"Rigby," the overseer replied, holding out his hand to Garrett. He shook it with a shark's flash of a smile, virtually ignoring Perry, whom he obviously surmised to be Garrett's assistant and therefore not worthy of any attention.

"This is my partner, Detective Lowell," Garrett said, directing Rigby's gaze to her.

Rigby's smile slipped as he hastily offered his hand to her.

Then it was time for business. "I'm aware that your main industry is shipping, but rumor has it there's a handful of mechs you employ who do some finer work. I was wondering if you might have someone who could have done something like this?"

Rigby looked perplexed. "Yes, well, I'll send for Jamison. Mechanical limbs are outside my realm of expertise, however, he transferred out to the Southwark Enclaves for a year, and they deal exclusively in bio-mech and mechanical limbs."

He strode to the corner and pulled a lever. A throaty whistle screamed out through the factory and men lifted their faces to the overseer's office. Rigby spoke into the mouthpiece, "Jamison? To my office, please."

A man scrubbed his hands against his overalls and started toward the steps.

Rigby introduced them to Jamison, and explained what they were there for. He made as though to hover, but Garrett shot him a look. "Do you mind if we speak to Mr Jamison in private?"

Mechs were already second-class citizens; the man was unlikely to inform on anyone outside the trade, with his supervisor here.

"Yes, yes, of course." Rigby looked anything but pleased when he left, however.

"There's only a handful of men I know who could have made that," Jamison said, after a moment's silence. He traced his finger down over the rose template down the side of the thigh. "But this here tells me who it were. It's his signature. Puts a rose on all his work."

"Who?"

"The Maker," Jamison replied. "Works out o' Clerkenwell. Has a shop there, fixin' timepieces and the like, though that's just the front for his real business. Makes mech parts for people as can't afford the enclaves."

"And just how does a man have so much skill with mech parts? It's strictly forbidden for a mech to continue this line of work once he leaves the enclaves," Perry said, tracing the rose with her finger. "What's his actual name?"

"Not that we're interested in reprimanding him over

unsolicited enclave work." Garrett offered a smile. "We just wish to know more about the missing girl's mech leg. We're trying to establish potential motives for her disappearance."

Had someone realized that Nelly was a mech? Had they taken offense at it?

It was a weak line of thought, but all they had at the moment, and someone had to know something about Nelly's background - or who her family was. If there had been an accident, perhaps someone had brought her to the Maker to be fitted for a new leg? And who had paid for it?

Jamison considered the pair of them. One of the most difficult aspects of being a Nighthawk – a blue blood, but not one with any rights – was the distrust of the people. As far as the human classes thought, a blue blood was a blue blood, regardless of whether they were of the aristocratic classes, or simply a rogue who'd caught the virus by chance.

"Hobbs," Jamison said slowly. "James Sterling Hobbs. His da were a mech, which is how he learned the trade. When the enclaves refuse an application for a mech limb, he's someone a man can turn to. Sometimes does work for those who can afford his fees, that don't wish to wind up here." Jamison gave a tight smile. "Unfortunately, I didn't have the money to pay him."

"You're not a mech," Perry noted. "Unless I'm mistaken."

"No." Jamison tipped his chin to her. "Me wife caught the Black Lung. Needed a new chest pump to be able to breathe, but the cost were twenty years, in this prison." His voice dropped. "I got two bairns. Rigby agreed to transfer the debt to me. He ain't a bad sort, for all that. He'd prefer a big, strapping lad working his shifts, and my boys need their mother more than they need me."

"Do you have Hobbs' direction?" Perry asked.

With a sigh, Jamison wrote it down, then passed the slip

of paper across the desk toward them. He kept his hand on it. "You promise there won't be any trouble come of this? There's a lot of folk who don't end up in this here hell, because of men like Hobbs."

Sometimes being a Nighthawk meant balancing the needs of the law. If Garrett gave a damn about the Echelon, then he might have used this information, but after his youth on the streets, Garrett knew what it felt like to be crushed beneath the heel of the Echelon. The downtrodden human classes needed some sense of hope, or else there would be more riots and fighting in the streets. "You have my word."

He ignored the sharp look Perry shot him and took the slip of paper.

~

"YOU HAD no right to make that promise," Perry told him, as they caught the train to Clerkenwell. They'd shown their identity cards at the station, earning free passage. "You can't assure Jamison that no harm shall come of this. By law–"

"The only way anyone is going to know what Hobbs is up to, is if either of us tell them. I know I'm not going to speak of it. Are you?"

Perry subsided with a growl under her breath that sounded like she swore at him. "You're asking me to break the law. This is reportable."

"And all you'll end up doing is harming mostly-honest people who had the misfortune to be born to the human classes. It's a stupid law. The Echelon made it because they don't want anyone competing with their contracts. Hence, the poor get poorer and the rich grow richer. If you think I'm going to follow their edict, just because some rich lordling's pocket doesn't get lined, then you don't know me very well. I know you don't like to bend the rules..." She was so bloody obstinate at times, "but allowing this doesn't hurt anyone. Indeed, quite the opposite."

"Laws exist to protect society."

"If you believe that, then you should turn yourself in to the Echelon," he shot back, following in her wake as she stepped down from the train and fought her way through the crowd. "Females are most certainly not allowed the blood rites that make an aristocrat into a blue blood."

"I wasn't *allowed* to take the rites."

None of the Nighthawks were. Otherwise, they'd be dining in gilded dining rooms in the West End and not working themselves into exhaustion on the streets. "The point's the same. Females are unsuitable to the craving virus infection." He shot her a wry look. "Something about their gentler natures and hysteria and..."

Perry's glare could have shriveled chestnuts.

"I didn't make that law," he reminded her. "I know you're more capable than most of the Nighthawks we work with. More bloody-minded perhaps, but certainly capable. As far as I'm concerned, I don't think of you as female."

"Perhaps because I don't bat my eyelashes at you and simper. That's how women are supposed to act, is it not?"

Poor choice of words. "That's not what–"

"Perhaps I should take a leaf out of Miss Radcliffe's book?"

"What the hell is that supposed to mean?" He caught her wrist.

Perry spun, breaking his hold, her gray eyes spitting sparks. "Why don't you tell me?" The words were a dare, a challenge.

He ground his teeth together, seeing red. Back to the way

he'd handled Miss Radcliffe. *Christ.* He'd smiled, he'd flirt-ed... It was nothing he hadn't done with numerous female witnesses over the years. "Perhaps I'm not the one with the problem with Miss Radcliffe?"

Her jaw dropped. "*What*?"

"Are you jealous of her?" Perry's cheeks actually paled at his words and Garrett pursued the thought relentlessly. "Is it because she's everything that you're not? Is that what's stir-ring this insane train of thought?"

The moment the words were out he knew he might as well have used a knife. Her gray eyes widened and a flash of something - hurt - flickered over her face. Then they hard-ened. "Do you honestly think that I would want to be nothing more than some frivolous bit of muslin? Everything that I am, I've made of myself." She stabbed a finger into his chest. "I hunt murderers and thieves through London, and I'm damned good at it. Tell me that's not more important than curling my hair or...or butchering some needlework? Or perhaps you'd prefer it if I made my curtsies and bit my tongue and pretended everything you said was the most enlightened witticism I'd ever heard - which it's *not*, by the way. Perhaps you'd like me more if I simpered or... or flirted, or.... God only knows!" She threw him off, stalking ahead of him with hunched shoulders, as though he'd somehow wounded her.

Shit. Garrett started after her. "Perry, wait." If anything, her strides lengthened. "Perry." He grabbed her arm. "I'm sorry. That was uncalled for." He'd never been so unkind, but she'd touched a nerve and he'd cut back at her before he could think. "I like you just the way you are. You know that."

Her gaze slid away. "Of course you do. It doesn't matter. This is it. 291 Aplin Street."

"What?" He looked up in surprise.

"We're here," she repeated tonelessly, shrugging out of his grip. "Now, let me go. I've got a job to do."

"We," he corrected, following her. She hadn't forgiven him, he knew that, and he was still feeling a little pissed off himself, but they had a job to do now. It could be dealt with later, though he certainly wouldn't forget himself again and cast his words so carelessly. He shot her a sidelong glance. He felt like a right proper bastard, and she'd been the one who was challenging his professionalism.

Later. He let out a slow breath and knocked on the locked shop door.

There was no answer.

"Garrett," she murmured.

"Yes?"

"I think I can smell something. I think you ought to pick the lock."

A moment's work. The shop bell tinkled as she pushed her way through but the place was empty and silent. Garrett eased the door shut, then wrinkled his nose. His blue blood senses were nowhere near as acute as hers, but even he could smell the faintly rotting odour. It was nothing a human would have picked up, however.

"Jesus." He cupped his sleeve over his nose. "What is that?"

Perry had a handkerchief at her face. She tracked through the shop to the counter and peered over it. There was a trapdoor there - and a mess of blood spatter against the back wall.

"It's coming from below."

Their gazes met.

"You first?" she asked hopefully.

"Flip you for it." He tugged a shilling from his pocket and tossed it in the air.

As he clapped his palm over it, Perry called, "Heads."

It wouldn't take much to skew the results - he'd seen which way it landed and could easily use a bit of sleight-of-hand - but the memory of her shock outside as he laid into her, still haunted him. Garrett sighed as he lifted his hand. Tails it was.

"Bugger," he said, and swung his way down through the trapdoor.

Perry followed, shaking the small glimmer ball she'd brought with her. Its phosphorescent glow lit the interior of what looked like a storeroom. Eerie half-finished mechanical limbs hung in racks along the walls. Evidently, this was where Hobbs kept his side commissions. Out of sight and out of mind.

There was a pallet made up in the corner, with a pair of nestled blankets and a small stack of personal items, like children's books and toys. Garrett lit the candle down there and lifted it high. A body sprawled on the bed, though bloodied drag marks on the floor showed that it had been moved from upstairs.

The man looked to be at least two days dead, judging from the softening state of cadaveric rigidity. His arms were crossed over his chest and a pair of pennies gleamed over the closed lids of his eyes.

"Hobbs, I presume."

"What are the chances that he's been shot in the chest, just as an actress goes missing from the theatre?" Perry breathed softly.

"Interesting circumstances," he agreed. And that was what they had to look for. Patterns, coincidences... Anything unusual. "Looks like we're investigating two possible murders."

"Well, this one is definitely murder. Unless he ran into a

bullet at high-speed." Perry stepped cautiously around the pallet. "The door was locked and nobody would have seen his body behind the counter. Why move him down here?"

"It was done very shortly after he was shot too," Garrett noted. Otherwise they'd have never gotten his arms to cross like that.

He checked inside the man's shirt. Bruising darkened his right shoulder, but not the left. Tugging the man's shirt out of his pants, he checked the man's sides. Signs of *livor mortis* on his side, but though he'd been lying on his back, the skin there was pale, where the capillaries were compressed.

"He fell on his right side and lay there long enough for his blood to begin congealing. Could have been an hour or so. Not much longer I think, judging by the minimal extent of the discoloration on his side - and see here, where the majority of it indicates he spent most of his time on his back." Garrett sat back on his heels. "I doubt whoever moved him was the killer. It looks like he was shot and lay there long enough for *livor mortis* to begin setting in, but not *rigor mortis*. So somewhere between an hour and three hours after he was shot, somebody moved him."

"It could have been the killer," Perry argued. "He might have stayed around and shifted the body later."

"Then what was he doing for that first hour or so?" It usually took at least that long for signs of discoloration to begin mottling the skin.

She had no answer.

This was how they worked. Coming up with theories that the other would try to shoot down.

"They didn't alert the authorities, whoever they were," Perry said. "Why wouldn't they?"

"Perhaps they were protecting this." He gestured around the room. "Once the blue bloods of the Echelon realize he was crafting mech work on the side, they'll run an investigation into Hobbs."

"Or they panicked, or were threatened."

"Maybe they witnessed it," he suggested, looking up at her. "Maybe they knew the killer?"

"The interesting question is, just how well did Nelly Tate know Mr Hobbs? The link is definitely the leg - he must have crafted it for her at some stage, so she obviously had fittings with him."

"So either the work he does has some involvement with the case, or perhaps it's the connection between the two of them," he said.

"He could be her mysterious beau, perhaps. That makes more sense than someone killing mechs."

"She has a beau?"

"I suspect. The stagehands were telling me how excited she was to receive peonies on her birthday - when she receives roses and far better bouquets from her numerous admirers all the time. She's been receiving the bouquets once a month. They thought she had been walking out with someone."

"Hmm." Miss Radcliffe had said nothing about Nelly having an admirer - and women were usually alert to these matters. Though Miss Radcliffe had said that Nelly was close-mouthed about herself.

Perry reached for the stack of books beside the pallet-bed. "So, Hobbs was killed, then a day or two later - judging from the smell and the rate of decay - Nelly goes missing."

"Jealousy? We could be looking at a disdained suitor taking revenge on Nelly's lover."

"Could be something from her past too - perhaps a member of the mysterious family nobody knows anything about." Perry gently flipped the pages in one of the books.

"Or the mysterious person who moved Hobbs and placed him like this. Maybe Nelly had something to do with Hobbs' murder, so the witness goes after her?"

"You've been reading too many penny dreadfuls."

"Ha, ha," she said flatly. "Do you want upstairs or down here?"

He was still feeling guilty, damn her. With a sigh, he said, "The smell's not as bad for me. You take upstairs. And send a 'gram to the Guild so they can send the autopsy cart out to collect Hobbs."

3

Hobbs was bundled back to the Guild, so Perry and Garrett took a couple of hours to question the nearby business owners and go over the scene for anything else. Nobody had heard a gunshot, but with the bustling intersection outside, that could perhaps be explained away.

They took a brief swing by Hobbs' listed residence, but the place was cold and sterile. Nobody had been there for days and indeed the place looked like Hobbs spent most of his time in the shop. Time to get back to the Guild then.

Perry vanished the second they returned on some pretext of paperwork. Garrett watched her go. She despised paperwork.

Which made it evident she was avoiding him. Neither of them had mentioned the earlier argument, but it lingered in the room like some ghost. Lips thinning, he turned down into the depths of the Guild, toward the autopsy room and Fitz's dungeon. Doctor Gibson hadn't finished his autopsy - they'd put a rush order through - but from the sounds of gunshots, Fitz was in next door.

The tall, scrawny blue blood was the Guild's resident blacksmith-of-sorts, once it became obvious he couldn't handle anything gorier than a poisoning. For a man who took his blood with his tea, the sight of it tended to make him even paler than usual. If it was mechanical, however, then Fitz could tell you the make, model and purpose.

Garrett didn't bother to knock. The man was half-deaf anyway.

The testing room was fitted out like a shooting gallery. Garrett waved hello as Fitz saw him.

Fitz pulled the trigger and the target fluttered as the bullet hit the outskirts of it. He lowered the pistol and then tugged down the heavy sound-proofing earmuffs he'd designed. "That's the type of pistol used on Hobbs," Fitz called loudly, handing the pocket revolver to Garrett. "A Webley Bull Dog with a .442 Webley round. Gibson dug the round out of his chest an hour ago."

"That was quick."

Fitz shrugged. "Hardly a challenge, my friend. They're as common as muck."

A small, automated servant drone wheeled closer, hissing out steam. They were the sort of thing more frequently found in a merchant or aristocrats home, as a sign of affluence, but Fitz had long ago rescued this one from a pile of scrap and resurrected it.

Fitz set his earmuffs down on the tray it held, then handed a pair of bullets to Garrett. "So, how's the case going?"

Garrett loaded the bullets into the pistol and put one dead centre through the target. The Webley was in wide circulation, especially among the Royal Irish Constabulary, though better suited to short-range encounters. Small enough to hide in a coat pocket, which was part of its allure.

"Hobbs died immediately. Whoever did it, walked up to the counter and shot him over it. From the blood pattern, he didn't try to run, so either he wasn't expecting it or maybe the killer was a stranger? Someone he thought was a customer?"

Fitz stared at him, his freckles standing out in stark relief.

It must have been the mention of 'blood pattern'. Garrett sighed and put the pistol down.

"I'll try and estimate the distance the perpetrator was at when the shot was fired," Fitz said.

"Thank you."

A clatter in the corner announced the arrival of a message in the pneumatic cylinder system the Guild used. Fitz unfurled the paper, then passed it to him. "You're wanted upstairs. Lynch wants a report."

That was unusual. Garrett flicked a glance over it. Brief and to the point, much like Lynch, the guild master. "He usually doesn't bother to get involved in a case this early."

Unless there was a reason.

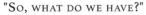

"So, what do we have?"

Sir Jasper Lynch, the Master of the Nighthawks, leaned back in his chair and surveyed the pair of them over the desk. Perry stood at attention beside Garrett, her hands clasped behind her. A thick wall of silence hung between them, and as she glanced sideways, she met Garrett's glance.

Though they'd barely spoken on the way home, they'd worked together sufficiently well. It was only now, with no dead bodies between them, that what had happened earlier reared its ugly head.

She certainly had no intentions of replying to that question.

"A burning curiosity about why this case is such a priority," Garrett finally replied.

Lynch pushed a piece of paper across his desk. "What do you know of Arthur Lennox, Lord Rommell?"

"We met him today. He's a part-owner of the Veil Theatre," Garrett replied, "I'm more interested in the theatre employees and what their relationship with Miss Tate involved, as well as trying to work out what happened to her."

"There's been no sign of the body yet, sir, or even any indication whether she's alive or dead," Perry added. "We've checked her home and none of her neighbours have seen any sign of her, though judging from the way she vanished from the theatre, I certainly don't expect her to have simply hurried home to fetch something."

"She was taken from the theatre?"

"So it seems," Perry replied.

"You mentioned Rommell?" Garrett prompted.

"Rommell's not just a financial backer," Lynch replied. "It's a particular interest of his."

"The theatre? Or actresses?" Perry asked. She knew what the blue bloods of the Echelon were like, only too well.

"Both." Lynch snorted, gesturing to the paper.

Garrett picked it up before she could and scanned it, his eyebrow lifting. He placed it back on Lynch's desk instead of giving it to her.

Petty. Perry's lips thinned, but she gave no other outward sign of irritation. Lynch was far too adept at reading people for that and he wouldn't tolerate arguments between the assigned partners on a case.

"That's... a considerable commission," Garrett said. "If

Rommell put it up himself, as reward for her return, then I'm wondering what the precise relationship between he and Miss Tate was."

So that was the push for priority on a missing person's case. Private commissions were accepted by the Nighthawk Guild, but the rate structure was often exorbitant. That served to prevent aristocratic blue bloods from demanding that their missing bracelet be placed above a murder case - which was entirely likely - but it also meant that when one of the Echelon did offer a commission, then it had to be given a certain priority.

"Do you have any leads at all?" Lynch asked.

"By all accounts Nelly Tate was well-liked," Garrett answered. "We've questioned the acting troupe, and nobody seemed to hold any animosity toward her. For the lead actress, she was rather more considerate than most, it seems. Miss Radcliffe, her understudy, said that Nelly had been helping her with her lines, which is almost unheard of."

Perry hesitated and Lynch saw it.

"Yes?" he turned to her.

Garrett stiffened at her side.

"Nothing, sir."

Lynch looked between the pair of them. Perry stared at the wall above him, her face impassive. The seconds tripped by, highlighted by Lynch's clock. If he expected either of them to break, then he underestimated their experience in handling him.

"Very well." Lynch's voice was so smooth it was clear he didn't believe her. "If there's nothing else to add... then you're dismissed."

Perry relaxed and turned toward the door.

"Oh, and Perry?"

She turned.

"Trust your instincts," Lynch told her, before giving her a brisk nod. "Whatever they might be."

Garrett shot her a dark look as she escaped through the door.

4

G arrett found her in the training room; the sound of grunts and striking blows drawing him down the corridor. They'd parted ways after the debriefing in Lynch's office, and Perry had used the distraction of several Nighthawks to slip away from him.

Perry's eyes flickered to his as he entered the room and Byrnes, one of his fellow Nighthawks, used the distraction to kick her in the chest. She staggered back, her fists coming up defensively and a scowl darkening her face.

They'd be at this until one of them cried uncle, which, knowing the pair of them, could be hours.

"Show me what you've got, princess," Byrnes taunted.

Perry's eyes narrowed and she launched into a stinging series of blows that Byrnes barely deflected. The other man's eyes were watchful though, and Garrett could see where Byrnes was goading her into an attack. She extended her punch a fraction too far and Byrnes was on her, flipping her over his shoulder and driving her down onto the mat. He yanked her arm up behind her back and ground the flat of his palm between her shoulder blades. Perry's eyes blazed with fury at herself – and no doubt a little bit of it for him.

"Can I step in?" Garrett asked.

Byrnes looked up. They'd never been friends – Byrnes had an edge of coldness that Garrett didn't entirely trust, and in return Byrnes saw Garrett's unwillingness to hurt a sparring partner as a weakness – but they often worked together as part of the ranking officers of Lynch's Hand.

"Ready for a rest, Perry?" Byrnes asked, letting her shoulder out of the lock.

"I wasn't referring to her," Garrett corrected.

Byrnes looked between them. Perry froze on her hands and knees, then seemed to gather herself as she stood. "Go on," she said to Byrnes. "I'll claim a rematch later."

"Might just stay and watch this one," Byrnes said, no doubt picking up on the tension.

"I'd suggest you don't." Garrett stared him down, pushing past him onto the mats that padded the sparring floor. He stripped off his coat, flinging it behind him, toward a chair, then started working on his waistcoat.

That set curiosity burning in the other man's eyes, but after another slow look, he melted away, shutting the door to the training room behind him.

Garrett locked it.

When he turned, Perry was still standing in the middle of the mat, her knees softened and her feet set defensively.

"I told you we needed to discuss what happened today."

Perry tipped her chin up. "Is that what this is? A discussion?"

"Maybe." He smiled. It wasn't nice. "Later."

Her eyes turned smoky and dangerous. "Then get your boots off."

"With pleasure."

The very pleasantness of the conversation belied the fury surging beneath his skin. It had been bad enough with her questioning his actions in regards to Miss Radcliffe, but that moment in Lynch's study... She'd let Lynch see her doubts and knowing *the* Nighthawk himself, Lynch wouldn't let well enough alone until he knew what the matter was. Lynch had the tenacity of a dog at a bone once he realized someone was keeping secrets.

Rolling up the sleeves on his shirt, Garrett discarded his boots and stepped onto the mat. This... this was exactly what he needed. The hunger of the craving virus lit through his veins, igniting his anger. It took quite a lot to push him to this point, but Perry had touched a nerve. If they wanted to sort this matter out so that they could work together, then he needed to deal with this now, regardless of her feelings on the matter. Knowing her as he did, she'd much prefer to pretend nothing had happened and skulk off to her room to nurse her grudge.

They touched fists, then separated. Garrett's knees softened, his eyes watching her like a hawk. The martial arts that had come from the Orient were taught to all of the novices, but when they sparred, all bets were off. It was a combination of pugilism and bartitsu, plus wrestling moves. Garrett knew his strengths as well as he knew hers. Perry would try to keep her distance, whilst lashing in for devastating blows. She was quick, but she knew enough to keep out of the circle of his arms, as he was much stronger than she.

He worked her lightly at first, dancing forward, then retreating when she went on the attack. It helped get the blood flowing in his veins and he knew she was holding back until his muscles had heated.

"Let's dance," Garrett told her, when he felt he was ready.

He took the attack directly to her.

If she was surprised by the onslaught, then she didn't show it, fighting grimly to keep him at a distance.

He rarely pressed her this hard in their sparring sessions, nor any of the other Nighthawks for that matter. Sometimes these sessions could get careless, and Garrett had never desired to hurt someone just for the sake of a match. Perhaps because he'd grown up in the streets of the East End, near Bethnal Green, where people didn't fight for entertainment or to enhance their skill.

There, it had been man pitted against man, for blood, coin or survival. Garrett had learned how to fight and to kill at an early age, and he didn't see the point of winning a bout here at the Guild. It earned you nothing, ultimately, though Byrnes and Perry, and some of the others didn't see it that way.

Perry's eyes narrowed and she danced out of the way as he lunged forward, the heel of her foot whipping toward his throat. Anger bubbled beneath the surface, and he met her, blow for blow. Faster. Harder. A writhing, graceful dance that earned a grunt here and there, and would leave the pair of them blackened and bruised by morning.

"This is... ridiculous," she panted, ducking and weaving.

"Really?" he snapped, drawing her into the cage of his arms and trapping her there in a lock. "Well, I'd have preferred to simply discuss the matter, but you kept retreating. So, let's not talk about it. Let us simply get this out of the way."

She broke free. "Fine," she snapped.

"You said I was unprofessional." Both of his palms hit her at the shoulders, staggering her backward. Perry's face darkened and she slapped her arms up inside his, slamming a ringing blow to his right ear.

"You were," she snapped. "A pretty blonde caught your eye and that–" A punch to the face that missed, "–was the end of any rational discourse."

"My interest in Miss Radcliffe is the same as any other male's. She's a beautiful young woman. She's clever and polite... Perhaps you should try that last one more often?" He was moving before he thought, one hand a distracting strike to her face that missed, whilst he slammed an open-handed blow against her abdomen. "But that's all it is." The movement was so natural he didn't realize how hard he'd hit her, until she crumpled over it, staggering back.

Bloody hell. He'd never intended to truly hurt her. The heat drained out of his face and Garrett took a step toward her, "Are you all–"

A narrow eyed glare was all the warning he got. Perry launched herself at him in a flying leap, her thighs locking around his throat. The momentum caught him off guard, and she flipped low, sending him crashing to the mats. Garrett rolled free, narrowly avoiding a punch to the face, but he didn't retaliate.

"Polite?" she snapped. "How about this? Fair warning, sir, I'm about to incapacitate you." A knee drove up between his legs, and he twisted out of the way, taking it to the hip, instead of the balls.

That did it. Garrett rolled to his feet with a snarl, fists held up to block the next punch. She was on him, punching and striking.

The strike to the balls had been a clear warning. If he was going to back down with her, then she would make him regret it.

Garrett backed away, holding up his hand to indicate a cessation. Perry instantly stilled. He flipped open the top button on his shirt, then dragged the entire thing over his head and threw it toward the rest of his clothes. He caught just a glimpse of her face as he tossed the shirt aside – a frozen, almost hunted look – before she smoothed her expression.

"First to cry 'mercy'," he warned. Usually their bouts ended with him giving her a nod and a cheery "good fight."

As if understanding the sudden seriousness of the matter, her eyes narrowed and she moved her right foot back, fists held up in front of her. A defensive position again, which was interesting. Maybe she knew she'd been in the wrong?

They went at it again, hands and feet flying. Garrett caught her foot, locking it against his thigh.

"This... is ridiculous," she snapped. "We barely argued."

"Really?" He twisted her foot, and her eyes widened as she realized what he was about to do. "And Lynch? That moment in his office? *'Trust your fucking instincts, Perry...'* Would you care to explain that? Or perhaps you'd prefer to speak to him about it, to tell him how you think I crossed the line, with a potential suspect?"

"I–"

The words died as he took her down. Perry kicked at his grip on her foot, but he twisted her ankle, forcing the rest of her body to roll with it, until she was flat on her stomach. She tried to gain her hands and knees, but he jerked her foot back, dragging her down again. After a mad scramble, he rolled her onto her back, his legs pinning her thighs. The second she tried to sit up, he slammed her back down.

"I didn't cross the line," he snarled.

"Does Miss Radcliffe think the same?" she shot back hotly, glaring up at him. "You don't even know the effect you have on women!"

Garrett pinned her, breathing hard. Fuck, she was

strong. He fought her as she tried to break free, but his weight was too much for her, his bare chest pressed against the leather protective corset she wore. "Say it," he demanded. "Say 'mercy'."

"Bugger. You."

Stubborn bloody chit. Perry strained, and Garrett let his grin show as she realized that his weight was too much for her to shift. He enjoyed every second of her frustration, until she finally slumped back in defeat, her gaze dropping away from his, and her breathing quickened.

He certainly wasn't letting her go, however. Not until she said the words.

They lay there for long seconds, breathing almost in unison. He could feel her chest straining against his. No doubt he was getting heavy, but she wore that mulish expression he hated so much. It often meant an argument he wouldn't win, but this time he wasn't backing down.

Come on, you stubborn chit. Just say it. "One little word, my lady peregrine."

Perry squirmed. Whatever she saw in his expression made her lips thin as she collapsed again. "Mercy." She spat the word.

"I'm sorry? Did you say something?"

If looks could kill... Perry's gaze incinerated him. "Get off me. I concede."

He could feel the fight leaving her, the muscles in her wrists slackening. Rather than straining against him, she softened, his hard body sinking into hers. He'd always known she was lean and lightly muscled, but it was somewhat of a surprise to realize that there were faint curves there, beneath the hard planes of his own body.

Garrett let go of her wrists, lifting himself off her. He

hovered there, however, the muscles in his biceps flexing effortlessly. "We're not finished with this discussion."

Then he pushed up onto his knees, kneeling over her. Her thighs were trapped between his. She didn't like it, her expression carefully blank as she levered herself up onto her elbows.

"Get dressed," she said. "I'm not arguing with you in these... circumstances."

Garrett rolled his eyes. The men often fought bare-chested. Clothing could get ripped or torn in the bouts, and Lynch kept a tight rein on uniform expenses. It also gave your opponent nothing to hold onto. "Christ, it's not like you haven't seen a man with a bare chest before."

That earned him a searing look. "It's indecent."

"I often am."

"You wish to discuss what happened today, with all these vulnerable areas showing?" Perry gave him the sweetest, evillest smile he'd ever seen. "Besides, perhaps you should save such a treat for Miss Radcliffe. *She* might appreciate it."

Garrett rolled to his feet. He didn't offer her his hand, turning to snatch up his shirt, and drag it over his head. Miss Bloody Radcliffe. It was starting to make the vein throb in his temples. "Anyone would think you a jealous wife. What is it about Miss Radcliffe that riles you so? Do you know her?"

"*What*?"

He glanced over his shoulder and let the shirt fall over the broad mass of his chest. "You didn't like her the moment you met her."

"I'm a trained investigator, Garrett, and she's the understudy of a missing actress. You tell me where my mind was going with that!"

"You've dealt with suspects before. You've never been like this."

"Maybe I'm not the one with the problem with Miss Radcliffe." She flung the words in his face, then turned and yanked at her coat, wincing slightly as she tried to fit her right arm through the sleeve.

He could have taken exception to her words, but he watched the way she favoured her arm. She'd never admit it, but it was hurting her, and now that he'd let out the force of his anger, it was finally burning low, like oil poured on a fire several minutes beforehand. Watching her struggle with her leather coat didn't make it easier to hold onto his fury. He couldn't shake the feeling that if he hadn't been so angry – if he'd controlled himself better – then she wouldn't be hurt.

Fuck.

Garrett stepped up behind her, catching hold of her wrists.

"What are you doing?" Perry demanded.

"I wrenched your shoulder, didn't I?" He stroked his hand over her right shoulder. "Let me ease the muscles."

Perry subsided with a growl, letting him draw her arms behind her in a stretch. Tension hardened the line between her shoulder blades, as if she didn't quite trust him so closely behind her.

"Relax." Garrett slid his hands up her arms, forcing her shoulders to drop and giving the tight muscles there a squeeze.

"I thought you were angry with me?" She tipped her head forward as he dug his thumbs into the smooth line of her trapezius. With every circle of his thumbs, tension dissolved in the muscle, and she made a faint murmur of pleasure.

Garrett let out the breath he'd been holding. He knew

how to melt a woman beneath his touch; he'd have never realized, however, that Perry was just as vulnerable as any other woman to that particular ministration. She made such a strong case of being just as capable and tough-natured as the rest of the Nighthawks, that he'd rarely seen a softer side to her.

"I'm still angry, but we have to work together." And it was a mild rasp along his nerves now, not a blazing inferno. A good fight was almost as physically relaxing as a hard fuck. The same sleepy lassitude rode through his body. "I'm angry that you thought I overstepped the line with Miss Radcliffe. I know where that line exists. I smile and flirt a little, because it puts female suspects or witnesses at ease." He clapped his hands over her shoulders and dragged her close enough to whisper in her ear, "Perhaps you should attempt such an approach. There's a reason I handle most of our interrogations. You can catch more flies with honey than vinegar."

"Is that what this is?"

"What?" He tried to peer at her expression.

"Forget it." Perry scowled and moved away from him, his hands falling from her shoulders. "I never said you weren't good at what you do, and I'm well aware of my own limitations, thank you very much."

She'd looked uncertain though. There'd been something there that he couldn't quite read, and he'd long considered himself an expert on women. Perry however, was outside the realms of what he knew. She always had been.

Perry picked her over-shirt off the hook on the wall and slid her arms into it. When she looked up, there was no trace of whatever he'd seen on her face, but he knew he'd not forget it.

"No," he said slowly. "But you intimated that I stopped

being professional." He could still hear the crack of the lecture Lynch had given him all of those years ago, when he was a novice.

She arched an eyebrow.

"Fine," he snapped. There was no point arguing with her anymore. "We'll agree to disagree. But next time, you can handle Miss Radcliffe."

"Perhaps I will."

The sound of her words followed him through the door, which he slammed, just a little.

5

Some women—like Perry—looked ghastly while crying.

In others, it brought only a rosy bloom to already creamy cheeks and made the limpid pools of their eyes look even bluer. Of course, Miss Radcliffe was one of the latter group.

Perry sank into the chair opposite the woman, well aware that Garrett was watching from the door, with his arms crossed over his chest.

Next time, you can handle Miss Radcliffe, he'd snapped. It hadn't been an idle threat.

"So tell me about the flowers," she suggested. An uneasy sensation made her stomach squirm. She hadn't been handling this case well at all, and Miss Radcliffe wasn't to blame for that. And whilst she genuinely felt sorry for the blonde actress, Perry knew she wasn't very good at handling grieving people. That was more Garrett's forte than hers. Easy for him to say you could catch more flies with honey, but he had a natural charm she could never hope to mimic.

Miss Radcliffe's eyes kept flickering between them, as

though even she could sense the tension. It was utterly humiliating.

"Red roses," Miss Radcliffe sniffled into her delicately patterned handkerchief. Her message had arrived by pneumatic tube that morning, requesting a word with Garrett. "Two dozen of them. They always arrived for Nelly before her big shows." A wave of wetness coursed down her cheeks as she looked up, her eyes betraying a hint of fear. "They arrived for me this morning with a note. I haven't let anyone touch it, but it's the same person who's been sending them to Nelly. Do you think...? Do you think it's the man who took her?"

Garrett strode toward the flowers in their vase, and examined the note. "*For your upcoming debut as lead. I look forward to it, my dear. You shall be a shining jewel among the masses.*" He flipped it over, but there was nothing on the back.

"It could simply be an admirer," Perry said awkwardly. Should she reach out and pat the woman's hand? Such a display was uncomfortable but Garrett often touched people. It put them at ease.

"But they knew I've been offered the lead." Miss Radcliffe suddenly flushed, as though realizing how that sounded. "Just until Nelly's back. Mr. Fotherham said the show must go on. How could someone know that? Only the theatre staff are aware. They don't have time before tonight's show to change the playbill!"

Perry made a decision. "Even if it is the abductor–" She was loathe to call it a murder, until Nelly turned up in one way or the other, "–both Garrett and I shall be in attendance. Nothing's going to happen to you tonight. And... And Garrett shall see you home safely afterwards." That would help this situation, wouldn't it?

Garrett had been correct. For whatever reason, Miss Radcliffe's mere presence made Perry uncomfortable in a way she'd rarely experienced before. Was it jealousy? Of what though? Miss Radcliffe's simple ability to be utterly charming, stylish and clearly well-bred?

She's exactly what you tried to be as a young girl, a voice whispered in her head. *And what you failed at.*

Maybe Garrett was right? Maybe her gut reaction did have something to do with jealousy?

Good God, was *she* behaving less than professionally here? After accusing him of the same?

It was an ugly thought.

"Do you know who delivers the flowers?" Perry asked, flipping open her notepad. "We could perhaps trace them back to the owner."

Facts were easier than emotions. Miss Radcliffe wasn't entirely certain, as the youth who made the deliveries to the theatre was unknown to her, but she did offer a description, and she knew what time the lad arrived each day.

"Thank you for your co-operation." Perry stood, tucking her notepad in her pocket. "We should leave you to prepare for the night ahead. We'll follow up on the flowers tomorrow at noon, when the delivery lad arrives."

Garrett was smiling at Miss Radcliffe when she turned toward the door. "Break a leg tonight. That is the correct expression, is it not?"

Instantly Miss Radcliffe relaxed. "Thank you." She took a deep breath, a small glitter of excitement glowing in her eyes. "It was a positively horrible dress rehearsal, which means tonight's show should be spectacular." Then she sobered. "Oh, I shouldn't even be thinking such a thing when poor Nelly is... missing."

"Leave Nelly to us," Garrett told her. "People don't just

disappear. We'll find her, for you. You just concentrate on the show."

They left Miss Radcliffe nervously murmuring her lines.

Garrett's smile lasted only so far as several feet along the corridor. "I'm walking her home, am I?"

"She feels more comfortable with you" The corridor seemed narrow and hot all of a sudden, and Perry's strides were brisk. "Perhaps it would be best for us to separate? There's something bothering me about Hobbs' murder. I want to go back through his books, see if there's any reference to Nelly or her amputation in his ledger. There has to be some sort of connection between the pair of them."

"And you want me to remain here?" Garrett's shoulder brushed against hers as they reached the bottom of the stairs, leading up to the back of the stage.

"Someone needs to keep an eye on the theatre." Perry shrugged. "The flowers bother me. Whoever sent them has turned his attention from Nelly to Miss Radcliffe quite quickly."

"You think someone removed Nelly from the show to make way for Miss Radcliffe?"

"Always a possibility. It could mean she's in danger too. Maybe Nelly rejected her suitor? Mrs. Fotherham said earlier that Miss Radcliffe bears a striking familiarity with Nelly." This was the frustrating part of a case: dozens of tiny little pieces floated before her, none of them fitting together in a nice, orderly pattern. She needed more information, more clues - the missing pieces to the puzzle. To keep digging until she found something that tied the pieces together, and she could put a working theory into place. "But I'm not quite sure how Hobbs fits into that, and I need to find out - I think he's the string tying this whole thing together. Maybe you could examine Nelly's room again? Try and work out how she could have disappeared without anyone noticing."

"I don't like you working alone."

"We often work alone," she retorted. "And I'm perfectly capable of handing someone his teeth, if needs be."

The faintest quirk of a brow. He was standing quite close to her, in the shadows of the theatre. Above them, dozens of stagehands scuttled around the stage, setting everything into place for tonight. "I've always found you more partial to a man's privates."

Perry colored up, and he noticed.

"As a target," he said wryly. "You're far more ruthless than I."

"That's only because you suffer an instinctive wince whenever you see a man downed in such a manner. I don't have that problem. Any vulnerability, any time."

He let out a soft exhale of a laugh. "Lynch's favourite motto." Then his expression sobered, and he added in a gentler tone, "Watch your back. If you haven't returned by three o'clock, I'm coming after you."

Perry rolled her eyes. For a moment it felt very much like their old sense of camaraderie - though she could still sense something lingering beneath the surface, between them.

Let's just pretend nothing ever happened.

"If you're not here by the time I return," she shot back, "I'll come rescue you too."

Garrett grinned and brushed his knuckles along her jaw. "Happy hunting."

"You too. Break a leg. Or don't," Perry said dryly. "You're too big of a lummox for me to carry around."

∿

THERE HADN'T BEEN a good chance to examine the Maker's shop in detail yesterday, what with the discovery of the body. Perry made certain she locked the door behind her, and eyed the trapdoor into the cellar. She wouldn't find any evidence of Nelly upstairs in the shop, she guessed. No, Nelly and her mechanical leg would be somewhere in Hobbs' paperwork below.

"Somewhere nice and dark and creepy," she murmured under her breath, sliding down through the trapdoor into the workroom below. She lit the lantern she'd brought with her, and its flame gleamed on the trays of metal implements and the mech limbs that had been already crafted. They weren't as finely made as Nelly's leg, and lacked the synthetic skin that she'd used to hide the metallic gleam.

Hobbs had been a meticulous record keeper, judging from the heavy leather-bound tomes on the shelves - if one counted on the work to be coded.

Taking several of his logbooks from the shelf, she flipped through them, her eyes straining as she sought to work out the code. Bloody hell, he must have been paranoid. A legitimate fear though, when one thought of the Echelon's enclaves, with their enforced registration of mechs. The blue bloods of the Echelon wouldn't like knowing that unregistered mechs moved throughout the populace without so much as a serial number or means of identification.

A further search brought her to a timber box, which opened to reveal some sort of cipher machine, or cryptograph. There were six wheels within it, each indented with copper letters and numerals she didn't know. She'd seen the type before, once, on a visit to the War Office, but this was outside her realm of experience.

There'd be a key that helped decipher the algorithms

used. Possibly the long line of text rotating on a cylinder above the copper wheels. Snapping the lid shut, Perry dragged it off the shelf. Fitz would know how to crack it, if necessary, and then Hobbs' secret ledgers would be available for her perusal.

Dumping it on the table, she gathered up the logbooks. There was a diary there too, more of a field diary, than a personal one. The notes were crude and rudimentary, and odd little scientific drawings had been tucked into the folds. Anatomical drawings of a child with strange cleft hands, and a cleft foot. A gap in its lip showed it's teeth, and Perry paused.

The drawing was titled, '*Lovecraft*'.

The next page detailed the finding of a child of monstrous proportions, who'd been abandoned in the alley behind the shop, and beaten by local children.

'*It is believed that Lovecraft's mother,*' the author mused, '*suffered a fright during her pregnancy of such proportion that it caused the mother to go into paroxysms. Hence, the child was born severely malformed. It is truly hideous to look at, and the local children all fear it, but I wonder at the malformations. Could I, with my skills, create limbs to replace the misshapen ones? Though the child tends to deafness, perhaps he could live a relatively normal life once the defective limbs are removed or enhanced?*'

A floorboard creaked above her. Perry froze, glancing upwards as she slowly eased the diary closed. She was just about to relax when a faint shifting whispered again. Someone stealthily slipping across the floor. Tiny little pinpricks marched down the back of her neck, and she eased out the breath she'd been holding.

Someone was in the shop with her.

She'd locked the door behind her. Perhaps they'd come

through the side door that led out into the little brick yard behind the shop?

A pair of pistols were strapped to cuffs around her wrists. She triggered the right one, and the wrist-pistol slapped into her palm with a faint click. Perry melted behind a stacked shelf with mechanical arms and legs hanging from it. The lamp on the other side of the room betrayed her presence, but there was no way she could bring herself to extinguish it. Darkness was the one thing she truly feared after that time as a young girl when–

-don't think of that–

Fear punched through her chest. It was too late. She'd given the monsters of her past a glimpse into her mind, and the familiar swirl of panic settled in her chest.

Damn it. She could barely hear over the thumping of her heart. Tingling started about her lips, and her mouth went dry. *Hell.*

She hadn't suffered a fit of hysteria in years, and she couldn't afford another now. Her protective over-corset seemed to tighten as if fingers dragged through the laces at back.

Identify the cause, Lynch's calm, familiar voice reminded her. *What is it you fear?*

They'd worked together over the years to manage her hysteria. The martial arts and meditation he'd recommended helped, but Lynch's true power was working out the rationale behind maladies of the mind.

I can't see him. She focused on breathing out, nice and slow. *I can't see who it is, and I'm trapped down here, the way I was when–*

She forced the past out of her mind. It had no place here, and the brief thought of it only made the sway of dizziness worse.

If she didn't move, she wouldn't be able to.

Perry swallowed hard, and forced her muscles to unlock. She was strong and powerful now, the way she hadn't been as a young woman, and her then-tormentor was gone. She'd never have to see him again. This wasn't the same. She was a blue blood now, with power.

But the not-knowing was making it harder to breathe. She had to see him.

Confront the fear, Lynch whispered in her mind.

Exploding up the narrow ladder, Perry squinted briefly against the glare of the light through the shop windows. The enormous shadow in front of her froze, hunching low, and as her eyes focused, she saw its hideous face widen in shock as she leapt over the counter and held her pistol up.

"Don't move." The tremble in her fingers betrayed her, but the pistol held steady. She wasn't alone in the dark anymore, and somehow that made it easier to breathe.

The creature was enormous. It towered over her by a good foot, with shoulders the size of a wine barrel, yet something about the way it hunched made her confidence soar. As if it was afraid of *her*.

Perry licked dry lips. "Stay right where you are. What's your name? What's your purpose here?"

Thick fingers flexed behind the creature's leather half-glove, revealing four thick fingers. She could just make the tiny clockwork whirring in the joints as they flexed. Not mech-made, but clock-mech, which was an older form of mechanism the blacksmiths had been able to devise. True mech work often joined seamlessly with flesh, but this was a stop-gap measure.

Clothes hung from its figure and someone, not too long ago, had cut the man's hair neatly, though lack of attention made it stick out beneath the cap he wore. His cheeks bore the burr of gingery fluff, though nothing grew on the scarred section of his upper lip. Brass earmuffs covered its ears, and she could almost hear the tinny vibration of her own words echoing within the contraption, with her superior blue blood senses.

"Lovecraft?" Hobbs' diary had said his lip was cleft, and he suffered from deafness, after all. Could this creature be the orphaned child he'd spoken of? "Can you hear me?"

The behemoth didn't move. One eye rolled, as though he was trying to see what she'd been doing below stairs. Nervous sweat trickled down his temples. Perry made a decision.

"I'm going to put my gun away," she told him, holding it up. "Please don't make any sudden moves. I just wish to speak to you."

The man backed up a step as she moved, his eyes trained on her pistol like an animal that knew when something could hurt it.

Perry slid it into her holster, and held her hands up in a placating gesture. "My name is Perry. I'm a Nighthawk, here to discover what happened to Hobbs. He was your... your friend, wasn't he?"

Wary blue eyes met hers. The man nodded, and made a sound that showed where his lip had been sewn together over what looked like a pair of fused metal teeth.

So, Lovecraft could hear her - or understand some of what she spoke of. Another glance at those clockwork hands promised that he'd had nothing to do with Hobbs' murder. He wouldn't be able to grip a pistol.

"Did you know Nelly Tate, the actress? Did she come here at all, to get her leg seen to?"

"Nerly," Lovecraft growled, but she couldn't be certain if

he was repeating her, or answering her question. He circled her warily, then disappeared down the ladder.

Perry hesitated. Returning to the dark made her feel somewhat less safe, but she didn't gain the feeling that man-child would hurt her, so she followed.

The behemoth limped across the floor, then lifted the mattress in the corner, and slid out a thin lacquered box. "Nerly," he said again, lifting the lid to show her.

There were photographs inside it; a seated man and a woman who stared unsmiling at the camera, with her hand resting on his shoulder. Scrawled across it were the words: *'To James, With Love, Nelly.'* There were also a whole string of playbills advertizing her in various theatre productions going back almost six years.

More photographs revealed the young actress, both at another theatre and smiling shyly in a park. One of them featured a young boy in short strings, with his hand clasped through a much-younger Nelly's, and a frozen look on his deformed face as he stared at the photographer.

Lovecraft. Perry looked up over the edge of the photographs, and put them gently back into the box. "Nelly and James were friends, weren't they? They've known each other a long time." Since Nelly was a young girl, judging by that last photograph.

He made a muffled sound, fingering the last photograph with a child-like wistfulness.

"Perhaps it would be best if you come with me," Perry suggested, setting a hand on his sleeve. From the smell of him, he'd been sleeping in alleys the last few nights. "I'll take you to the Guild. We can get you something to eat and drink, and perhaps a bath? Would you like that? Would you–"

He yanked his arm out from under her grip. "Nuh. Nuh.

Stay 'ere. Nerly." Fisting the enormous clockwork fingers, he curled them up by his face.

"Nelly's not going to come here again," Perry whispered. "Nor Hobbs. Do you understand that? Hobbs has... gone to sleep. Forever. You put the coins on his eyes, didn't you?"

That set him off. He pounded his fists against the brass muffs that covered his ears. Then again.

Perry tried to grab his hand. "Please don't, Lovecraft. You'll hurt yourself." She swallowed. "Come back to the Guild with me. Maybe you can help me find Nelly? If you answer my questions, I might be able to trace where she's gone. Maybe she's not sleeping, like Hobbs? Maybe you can help me save her?"

The big brute bared his teeth at her. "Nuh!" Agony twisted his ugly features. For a moment, Perry almost reached out again, at the look in those childlike blue eyes, but he shoved past.

Lashing out at her, he drove her back into the wall, and thundered toward the ladder. Perry caught her breath, then started after him, but he jerked the ladder up through the trapdoor and slammed it shut. The lock clicked home and footsteps hammered dust down between the floorboards. Then a door slammed.

Gone. He was gone.

Damn it. Perry glared up at the trapdoor. It was going to give her a devilish time, trying to get it open. And what in blazes did any of that interaction mean?

At least she now knew that Nelly had been a frequent part of Hobbs' life. Nelly must have visited often enough for Lovecraft to have formed some sort of affection for her, which meant the link was there. Hobbs' murder was directly involved with Nelly's disappearance.

She just had to find out how.

As soon as she got that damned trapdoor open.

THE THEATRE WAS a hive of activity.

Last minute costume changes had to be seen to for Miss Radcliffe, who was slightly taller than Nelly Tate had been, someone was screaming about greasepaint in the wings and demanding to know where the wig for Concetta was, and the lights were all blaring as the stagehands tested them.

Garrett used the cacophony to move about relatively unseen in the background. Nelly's dressing room was the last in the row, and somewhat isolated. He spent an hour examining the walls and mirrors in the room, trying to locate any hidden passages backstage. One door led to a storeroom filled with garish backdrops, but there was no sign of any other mysterious way in or out of that area.

Someone had to have seen her leave. Unless she'd not been missed in the chaos?

But if there was blood in her room, then she should have been injured. Surely someone would have noticed if Nelly had staggered out of her room, or even been helped out by someone else.

Garrett found a small, out-of-the-way alcove from which to watch the stage, while he waited for Perry. It wasn't long before a dark-figured blur stepped past the stage directly into the wings where he stood.

"Lord Rommell." Garrett tipped his head to the man.

Rommell looked less than pleased to see him, though he responded with a curt nod, and settled in beside Garrett. "How is the case progressing? Is there any sign of Nelly?"

While he'd questioned Rommell the day before, the man's sudden involvement in the reward for her return gave him a new lead to chase. "Unfortunately, there's been no sign of her. Might I ask about your involvement with Miss Tate? That's quite a substantial reward you've posted."

Rommell's attention seemed caught by something on stage. "Nelly was under certain contractual obligations to me. I ensured that she gained the role she desired, and was properly attired in jewels and clothes, and in return..." He gave a suggestive gesture.

"Ah." Nothing more needed to be said. Nelly had been Rommell's mistress. "Are you aware that flowers were delivered to her almost every week during her last run? Red roses. They didn't by chance come from you?"

Dark eyes glanced his way. "I'm not the only one with an eye for actresses. No doubt some of my peers sought to steal her out from under me. She was always receiving flowers. I cannot say she ever had red roses in her dressing rooms, however." He grimaced. "Had a thing for peonies, I believe. Received them every now and then, and they're the only damned things she'd keep. I can hardly fathom her interest, they're so cheap."

Not every woman liked the best that money could buy. Though he did frown a little. Nelly liked peonies, did she? It was the kind of thing someone of less-well-to-do-stature could afford. And she received them regularly? He'd thought they only came on her birthday.

Following the focus of Rommell's gaze, Garrett realized the lord was surreptitiously eyeing up Miss Radcliffe, which was curious. "You were sweet on her?" he suggested, though he didn't believe his own words. "Is that why the reward?"

"I want to damned well know where she is," Rommell growled. "She was *my* mistress, and I wasn't finished with her yet. If someone's stolen her out from under me, there'll be hell to pay."

"Why would you presume someone's stolen her?"

Rommell looked surprised. "Well, what else could have happened? Where else could she have gone? I'd given her the best role in this damned theatre, and more than enough coin to see her well in hand. She won't have run from that. But I have enemies, and those jealous enough of my success to make me wonder. If they managed to somehow snatch her out from underneath my nose, they'll be crowing to themselves about such a coup. I can't allow that to stand. No, you mark my words. You should be searching among the Echelon for one of my rivals. They'll have her. I'll bet fifty quid on it."

Nelly wasn't a piece of furniture, but it was clear that Rommell thought of her as little more than a possession. The roses, Garrett suspected, definitely weren't from his lordship.

After all, why buy a woman flowers when he'd already bought her? That type of thinking was clearly up Rommell's alley.

Garrett smiled tightly. "Perhaps you could see fit to furnishing me with a list of those who might wish you harm." A way to placate his lordship and see to it that all leads were pursued.

Rommell obviously thought he was the centre of his own little world, but some gut instinct made Garrett wonder. There was more to this than a petty squabble between blue bloods, and although it wasn't entirely unknown for this kind of thing to occur in the Echelon, it would certainly be frowned upon. Nelly might only be human, but most blue blood lords kept to strict societal rules dictating which type of women were to be thralls - those debutantes that made thrall contracts with lords, exchanging their blood rights for protection, clothing and jewellery - and those that the blue bloods could parade around on a leash as a blood slave. A slave had no rights, but most of those young women were sold from Newgate or other lowly establishments, upon committing a crime. Only rarely were they kidnapped off the streets, or out of a theatre.

That would be somewhat beyond the pale. And Nelly was too well known for her to be paraded around as a blood-slave.

"And if she doesn't return?" he asked.

"Mistresses come, then they go," Rommell replied. "You know how it is." He was watching Miss Radcliffe again, barely paying attention to Garrett.

"Not really. I don't need to pay for my women."

The insult was lost on the bastard. Rommell smiled. "Or perhaps you can't afford them, hmm?" He flicked at a piece of lint on his sleeve. "I imagine circumstances are rather straitened as a Nighthawk."

"I make do." It was none of the bastard's business about Garrett's relationships with women. Any of them. And he despised the way Rommell obviously thought them inter-changeable. Garrett *liked* women. He was still friendly with the majority of his ex-paramours, and found them mostly interesting and quite witty.

He simply hadn't found the right one yet. Someone who caught his breath, and made him forget every other young woman he'd ever met.

And speaking of young ladies... Garrett checked his pocket watch. Three O'clock, and no sign of Perry. He glanced at the stage, where Miss Radcliffe was discussing her cue with the director. Indecision gripped him. Stay here to keep an eye on the actress who'd received an interesting letter, or go after Perry?

She hated being coddled, and she was frighteningly proficient when she needed to be, but that didn't make it any easier to wait for her. If something had happened to her...

Rommell made the decision easier. The way he was watching poor Miss Radcliffe was practically proprietary. It made him feel ill to watch.

"If you'll excuse me," he said to Rommell. Miss Radcliffe was safe for the moment, with so many eyes upon her.

And Perry - practical, punctual Perry - was late.

PERRY BALANCED on the table she'd dragged under the trap-door, and concentrated on slipping the thin metal file she'd found below, between the crack in the trapdoor. It was frustrating work trying to unlatch the lock from this angle, and her lantern was rapidly burning down.

The bell above rang, and she froze as footsteps entered the shop.

Lovecraft? Or someone else?

Perry slid the file back down silently, trying not to betray her presence. Then the unmistakable scent of Garrett's cologne caught her attention.

Her shoulders slumped. Thank goodness. Reaching up, she hammered on the floor. "I'm down here!"

A snort sounded. "Looks like I am rescuing you, after all. What shall you owe me for this, hmm?"

"I shall *not* punch you in the chest when you let me out," she promised, with a faint growl at the end of her words.

"Tempting... But I think you owe me more than that."

Perry pressed her hand against the timber beams, and grimaced. "What do you want?"

"The paperwork on this case is yours," he said smugly. "All of it."

Of all the rotten... Perry glared up through the floor. She despised paperwork. Most of the time Garrett took care of it when her perfunctory notes didn't meet with Lynch's approval. "I'll oil your guns," she suggested, instead.

"As well as the paperwork? That's considerably generous of you."

"*Garrett...*"

"Is that a promise?"

Silence. She thumped the trapdoor. "Yes. Fine. It's a promise. Get me the hell out of here."

The lock snicked and light flooded in, highlighting Garrett's broad shoulders, and devastatingly handsome smile. He rested one hand on his knee and reached out the other to her. "Well, this looks like an interesting story. Care to tell?"

Grabbing hold of his hand, she hopped up lightly, and he used his considerable strength to haul her out into the shop. Landing on her tiptoes left her somewhat unbalanced and she slammed a palm into his chest to keep herself from tumbling into his arms. There'd be none of that nonsense.

Though she felt heat spilling through her cheeks.

She'd always been aware of him as a man, but it was only recently - since the start of the case - that she'd begun to realize that perhaps it wasn't only the temptation to watch him, that she would have to guard. It was troubling, this... this sense of jealousy over a woman who'd caught his eye. More troubling to realize that she'd been feeling this way for a lot longer than she'd been consciously aware of.

"Well, I found who placed the pennies on Hobbs' eyes." She hurriedly explained about the meeting with Lovecraft, trying to ignore her feelings. "Hobbs and Nelly have known each other quite a long time."

"Nobody seems to know her true name," Garrett replied. "I've been asking around. As far as the theatre is aware, Nelly's her stage name, but it's also the only one they know her by. So no use trying to track where she came from before she joined up a year or so ago, damn it."

"We'll see if we can track Hobbs' people then. There might be some relation between them. Or perhaps he was her beau?"

Garrett grimaced. "Actually, I believe that honor belongs to Lord Rommell. Or at least, he was paying her to be his mistress."

"Really?" Of all the people for Nelly to accept... Perry screwed up her nose. "Come on. There's a cryptograph downstairs I want Fitz to have a look at, and Hobbs' ledgers. Maybe there shall be some mention of Nelly there, once we've decoded them. You can help me with some of the heavy lifting." Tapping his biceps, she added, "It is what you're good for, isn't it?"

"I also think occasionally," Garrett replied, lowering himself through the trapdoor. "You stay up here, and I'll pass up what you need. No point both us getting locked below if your handsome friend happens to return."

"True." Perry's smile died as he vanished through the trapdoor. She was feeling a little breathless again, and somewhat weary of trying to keep a smile on her face when inside she felt like a tumultuous mess when he was around.

What in blazes was she going to do about this?

6

Applause erupted through the theatre as the actors took their bows.

Garrett idly scanned the crowd.

The play's first night had been a smashing success. Though both he and Perry had been in attendance - just in case - there'd been nothing to indicate anyone taking an unnatural interest in Miss Radcliffe. Rommell had reigned supreme, up in the boxes, and the director and his staff had rushed about like a stirred anthill.

"What do you think about that?" Perry murmured, her eyes locked on something up in the boxes.

Rommell's box, to be precise. The theatre was emptying as people streamed toward the exits, but several other aristocrats had joined Rommell. He appeared to be in a heated argument with one of them, stabbing a finger in the man's face and snarling.

Interesting.

"I'll see if I can get closer," he murmured, and Perry nodded.

She didn't like confronting members of the Echelon.

Though he knew there were rumors of a female blue blood among the Nighthawks, both he and Lynch took care to keep her separated from those who might take offense at her gender. The Council of Dukes who ruled the city might not do anything about it... but one couldn't take that risk. Being a rogue blue blood was a stiff hand to play in life, but Garrett knew that he wasn't in danger of being executed, or used as an example. Perry however...

"Watch your back," he warned.

"Always. I'll keep an eye backstage." She vanished into the crowd.

Servants in livery hovered outside the boxes as Garrett climbed the stairs. He paused outside the door to Rommell's box, listening intently.

"...you pompous fool. If I'd wanted to make a play for your mistress, then she'd be mine already." A sneering kind of voice. "I'd certainly set her up in higher standards than this–"

"You call that theatre you own a higher standard?" This from Rommell. He laughed. "Please, Miss Tate would have laughed in your face."

"Then why bother accusing me of stealing her away? If I'd wanted her, I'd have paraded her out of here right beneath your nose. You'd know all about it, Rommell."

Rommell's voice darkened. "I know you offered her a place at the Highcastle! I saw the note, don't you dare–"

There was a scuffling sound, and then someone else cracked out: "Gentlemen, please."

The door jerked open, and Garrett stepped behind it as someone stormed out of the box, a theatre cape swirling around his legs as he stalked toward the stairs. The man didn't even bother to look behind him, and Garrett set out in pursuit.

Outside the theatre, the fellow paused on the steps, and tugged his cheroot case from his coat pocket as he gestured a servant to send for his carriage. A match flared as he lit the cheroot, and Garrett took his opportunity.

"My lord?"

The fellow looked up. His eyes were a pale, pale blue, and his skin ashen, a sign that revealed high craving virus levels. The longer one was afflicted with the craving virus, the paler their coloring became, until they hovered on the verge of the Fade: a moment in time when the craving virus finally overwhelmed a man and they became something more... Something entirely predatory, and driven only by the thirst for blood.

Vampires had torn apart the city on more than one occasion. The Echelon had since decreed that a blue blood's CV levels were to be strictly monitored. The moment they reached seventy percent, the matter was to be reported to authorities as a risk. Any higher, and that blue blood faced execution, before they could begin to devolve into their vampiric state.

Whoever he was, Garrett suspected the fellow was staring the Fade in the eye.

"Garrett Reed, of the Nighthawks." He flashed his identification and Nighthawk badge, gaslight gleaming off it. "A word, if I might?"

The lord froze, smoke curling around his nostrils as he slowly breathed out. "Harrison Cates, Lord Beckham. What do you want?"

"Miss Tate's disappearance." Garrett put the badge away. "You seemed to know something about it?"

Beckham exhaled smokily, almost a laugh. "Did Rommell set you upon me?"

"No, I overheard some of the conversation taking place upstairs."

The man shrugged. "Like I told Rommell, if I'd wanted to take his mistress from him, I would have. With the coin the Veil is sucking from his pockets, I could have bought her thrice over."

"You own another theatre?" Garrett jotted down the man's words in his notebook.

"The Highcastle." Pale eyes raked over the facade of the Veil, a twist curling his lips. "Somewhat higher class than this."

Until then, Garrett hadn't realized that a man existed who thought more highly of himself than Rommell did. "Yet, you attend the Veil tonight?"

This time, Beckham spread his hands. "Guilty as charged. I might have been stirring the pot with Rommell. I've no interest in his mistress - it's not like she's any connections or great wit - but it's a devilish fun time making him think I do."

"He spoke of a note..."

"Yes, I offered her employment, and certain other... benefits." A smirk. "Then I had it delivered when I knew he was around."

"You don't by any chance send her flowers?"

"I don't send any woman flowers. Not even my mother." A light gleamed in Beckham's eyes as if a thought struck. "Though, that would have been more convenient than attending so many lacklustre shows here, and Rommell would have suffered an apoplexy." He clapped a hand on Garrett's shoulder and laughed. "Thank you, my good fellow. That's utter genius."

There was nothing here to be gained. Garrett asked a couple more questions, then snapped his pocketbook shut.

Beckham's main interest seemed to belong to Rommell. Indeed, if asked, Garrett had little doubt the bastard would even know if Nelly were blonde or brunette. She was simply a checker piece in play between the two lordlings.

"That's all, thank you, my lord," Garrett said, seeing his lordship's horseless steam-carriage wheel up to the curb. The gilded sigil on the door reminded him of a weasel - somewhat appropriate considering who it represented.

"Glad to be of help. Cheerio." The lord waved behind him and hopped up into his awaiting carriage in considerably good humour.

Garrett turned away in disgust. Where the devil had Nelly disappeared to? Without a body, they had few leads, and every time he thought a new lead presented itself, it turned into a dead-end.

Unless they pursued the Hobbs angle instead. Perry's photographic find today had offered more proof of a relationship of some sort there, than anything else. He was convinced the two cases were connected.

Now, he just had to discover what had happened to poor Nelly.

GARRETT WALKED through Miss Radcliffe's small three-room apartment and then turned and nodded at her. "It's clear."

Miss Radcliffe had been hovering in the doorway whilst he performed his search. "Thank you for walking me home," she said, brushing a lock of hair behind her ear. "I truly do appreciate it."

"Part of the job," Garrett replied with the type of insincere, professional smile that was easy to call up. Damn Perry, but he felt uncomfortable here, when he shouldn't. She was the one who'd suggested he walk Miss Radcliffe home, and though he wasn't doing anything wrong, he felt like he was.

All because of their argument.

"I'll leave you to it, Miss Radcliffe," he said. "If you need us, please send a note to the Guild. I've checked the locks - you should be safe tonight - but don't hesitate to call upon us, if something unnerves you."

"Eliza," she corrected, her hesitant gaze meeting his. "You may call me Eliza, if you wish. And thank you."

Garrett turned toward the door, but she caught his sleeve. He glanced down. "Yes?"

Furious heat bloomed in her cheek and she clutched her violet colored coat tight to her front. "Thank you. Again." Somewhat awkward and sweet. He knew what she was intending to do almost before she acted.

Miss Radcliffe reached up, and pressed her lips against his cheek. The faint scent of her perfume enveloped him and his body tensed, desire bubbling just beneath the surface. If he turned his face, he'd be able to brush his mouth against the trembling pulse that was visible in her throat, perhaps even nip her there. It aroused the darker side of his nature, the part of him that was purely a predator. A blue blood was always tempted by thoughts of blood and sex, though he'd found his own hungers manageable in the past.

But then, Perry had been pissing him off lately. He was already on edge, and strong emotions only exacerbated the hunger's grip.

Thoughts of her acted like a dash of cold water to the face.

He withdrew, clearing his throat. "Miss Radcliffe–"

"Eliza," she insisted, her dark eyes shining in the candle-light. So damned tempting...

Garrett shot her a rueful smile. "Perhaps after this is done, I might call you 'Eliza'. Until then... it wouldn't be very professional of me."

Despite the toll the last two days had taken upon her, she drew back and nodded, understanding him perfectly. "And when this *is* done, Detective Reed?"

Their eyes met.

He shouldn't. It would only reinforce Perry's suspicions of his handling of this case, and that irritated him. Damn her to hell. He was handling this as professionally as he could. He was entitled to his own diversions, in his own time... and Miss Radcliffe was lovely, intelligent and intriguing.

He shouldn't encourage this. He knew he shouldn't. And yet he couldn't help picturing Perry's stern, disapproving face in his mind when he leaned closer and murmured, "Perhaps, when this is done, you might be available to show me more of the theatre. As an audience member, instead of actress?"

Perry was a spur he didn't need, but a part of him wanted to blandly look her in the eye after the case was finished, and tell her that he intended to take Miss Radcliffe out to the theatre. To dare her to say anything about it.

Miss Radcliffe smiled sweetly. "Until then, Detective."

"There he is," Garrett murmured the next morning, nudging Perry's arm and tipping his chin toward the young lad who was making his flower deliveries.

The young boy had adapted a pneumatic steam-powered rickshaw into a flower cart that he could ride, and as they watched, he swung his leg off the seat and wheeled it up onto the kerb outside the theatre. He tipped his cap to the stagehand waiting for the delivery, his grin faltering when he saw the pair of them step out of the shadows near the back alley.

"A word, if we might?" Garrett asked, with a smile to set the boy at ease.

"Aye, what can I help you with?"

"You often deliver red roses for Miss Nelly Tate. Do you know who puts that order in?"

The lad scratched his head. "Pick 'em up from Welham's Florist. You'd have to ask him. He's the one as takes the orders."

Excellent. Garrett and Perry moved off, following the

directions the boy gave. For the first time, Garrett felt as though they had a solid lead upon which to follow. Nelly received flowers all the time, but only two posies were sent to her regularly, which indicated someone – or two some-one's - with a particular interest in her.

Welham's was set in the heart of the theatre district, where it did prime business. Flowers loomed and dripped from vases as they entered, and there was an air of sophisti-cation and entitlement to the shop. Indeed, the man behind the counter examined them with a faintly arched brow as though wondering what they were doing there.

Garrett introduced them, flashing his credentials. "We're curious about an order of red roses that is sent weekly to Miss Nelly Tate at the Veil Theatre. Or more particularly, we're interested in the name of the person sending them."

Welham pressed his wire-rimmed spectacles up his nose. "A standing order for red roses? Yes, I know the one. A Mr. Hobbs, I believe. Once a week the order is to go through."

"Hobbs?" Perry blurted. "James Sterling Hobbs?"

Welham looked surprised. "Yes, that's the one."

Roses weren't cheap, but then, they already knew that Hobbs was making a small fortune from his side business.

"And is there a frequent order for peonies?" Garrett asked.

Mr. Welham shook his head. "Goodness, no. That's the sort of thing you can buy in Covent Garden."

Thanking Mr. Welham for his time, they turned toward the door. The bell rang as it shut behind them.

"Who sends the peonies then?" Perry asked, as soon as they were alone. "I felt certain they must have come from Hobbs. One of the stagehands seemed to think she was terribly excited to receive them. The roses however... Nelly kept them, but she didn't seem to make as large a fuss over them."

There went their lead. A dead end, like all the others. Garrett swore under his breath. "Rommell and Hobbs were both interested in her, for their own reasons. So was Lord Beckham, but he sent no flowers... I feel like we're missing something."

"You think there's someone else involved?"

"Maybe."

"We need to know what the connection is between Nelly and Hobbs," Perry said, "And who sent her the peonies."

"Back to the theatre?" he suggested. "We should see how Eliza is faring."

"Eliza?"

A slip of the tongue. Garrett met her gaze, daring her to comment. "Miss Radcliffe."

Perry's gaze drifted away. Sometimes that was worse than if she'd commented, for he had no idea what she was thinking at the moment. Muscles bunched in his gut in expectation, but the moment stretched out, and still she said nothing. "Cat got your tongue?" he asked.

Cool gray eyes locked on his. "No," she said coolly. "The theatre it is."

And that told him nothing at all, either, damn her.

GARRETT HAD GONE in search of the stagehand who'd originally commented on the significance of the peonies, leaving her to deal with Miss Radcliffe.

Or Eliza. Perry hadn't missed the significance of that little slip of the tongue. What had he meant by it? What had happened last night?

Don't, she told herself severely. She'd already made a muck of things. Time to focus on the case, and not on what had occurred between her partner and the beautiful actress, in the privacy of the woman's apartment.

No sign of Miss Radcliffe in her dressing rooms. Perry withdrew from the room with a frown–

"There you are!" Someone called.

She looked up as one of the stagehands bore down upon her, then glanced behind her. There was no one there, which meant he must be referring to herself. "Can I help you?" Recollection began to dawn; she'd begun to place names and faces here. "It's Arthur Millington, isn't it?" One of the stagehands.

"Aye. A man tried to drag Miss Radcliffe into a carriage not ten minutes ago," the man declared. "Right off the street!"

"Miss Radcliffe? Is she all right?"

"Shaken up and scared, but she ain't injured if that be what you're asking."

Good God. "Where is she?"

Millington gestured toward the stage. "Lord Rommell's with her. Saved her from the ruffian, thank the devil."

The sound of raised voices caught her ear as she hurried toward the stage. A pair of figures materialised; Miss Radcliffe and Lord Rommell, deep in quarrel at the side of the stage.

"–not to see that Nighthawk again," Rommell snapped, then his voice changed to a soft cajolement. "I can keep you safe, Eliza. There's no need to fear another assault, when I can have a man guarding your door during the day."

"And what of my nights?" Miss Radcliffe stammered.

Rommell lifted a hand to her cheek, his face tightening

when she subtly withdrew. "I'm certain we can come to some sort of arrangement there too."

"I–I–" Miss Radcliffe colored up, as if realizing she'd walked into a trap. "I spoke in haste. I'm certain that I'll be quite safe at home. My door has a sturdy lock upon it."

Something ugly flickered across his expression. "Hopefully, it's sturdy enough." He tipped his head to her. "Don't wait too long to consider my offer. You don't want to see it withdrawn."

Rommell stalked in the other direction, his back stiff, and Miss Radcliffe watched him go. When he vanished, she let out a tiny, quivering sigh, and whispered, "When hell freezes over, my lord." The moment she turned, she caught sight of Perry, her breath catching. "Detective." A fleeting glimpse of fear darkened her expression. "I didn't realize you were standing there."

Sympathy was a brutal crush in Perry's chest. Perhaps both she and Miss Radcliffe had more in common than she'd thought. She too had been at the mercy of a powerful lord once, though in entirely different circumstances.

But that sense of being alone, trying to deal with consequences you couldn't quite escape, and knowing that no one could help you... Oh, yes, Perry knew what that felt like.

"Here," Perry murmured, tugging a handkerchief out of her pocket, and presenting it to Miss Radcliffe.

"I'm so sorry." Miss Radcliffe dabbed at her eyes, a false, watery smile painted on her lips. "That was most unbecoming of me. I'm sorry you had to hear me say such a thing."

"Yes, well, it echoed my own thoughts somewhat." The dark stir of the craving virus lifted its head within her. For a moment Perry had a thoroughly enjoyable image of beating the claret out of Rommell. Heat flared behind her eyes, and

Perry swallowed hard, knowing they'd just turned black. "Rommell ought to be given the strap. What kind of man uses such an opportunity to hunt a woman into his own bed?"

"One without so much as a hint of nobility in his nature," Miss Radcliffe said, somewhat bitterly. Then she flushed, as though realising what she'd said.

"I'm not going to say anything," Perry murmured. "You may speak plainly."

Miss Radcliffe's shoulders slumped, and she worried the handkerchief in her hands. "He makes me feel ill."

"He makes me feel somewhat violent," Perry admitted.

That won her a faint hint of a smile. Miss Radcliffe looked wistful. "You're so brave," she said. "I wish I could be as accomplished and independent as you. I should like to be able to stand up to men with impunity."

Truly? Miss Radcliffe admired *her*? "It's not quite as easy as you make it sound," Perry replied carefully. "I hear that there was an incident outside, where someone tried to grab you?"

That washed away any hint of smile. Miss Radcliffe paled. "You don't think it was the same man as... as kidnapped Nelly?"

"I couldn't speculate. We don't yet know if it was a man or woman who had anything to do with Nelly's disappearance. Did you see who tried to grab you? How did you get free?"

"I was just trying to take some air in the alley behind the theatre, when someone grabbed me from behind," Miss Radcliffe replied. "I'm sorry, but I was so distracted that I didn't see anything - just a glimpse of his hands. He slammed one over my mouth so that I couldn't protest. I was certain that something was going to happen to me - that I was going to end up with poor Nelly, so I bit him, and managed to scream when he let go. Ned Barham - one of the stagehands - ran to help, and the man fled."

"Did Ned see what he looked like?"

Miss Radcliffe shook her head. "I don't think so. The fellow cast me aside when he ran, and poor Ned had to help me up. He didn't know what had happened, at first."

First, the red roses... and now someone had tried to assault Miss Radcliffe, perhaps even steal her away too. "It sounds like someone has an unhealthy fascination with actresses."

"Do you think they'll try again?"

"They may," Perry admitted. "Which is why you're going to take up Lord Rommell's generous offer of a man to watch over you during the day. I'll arrange for a Nighthawk to keep a watch on your apartment of nights, though, whilst we try to get to the bottom of all of this."

"And what should I tell Rommell?"

"Tell him it wouldn't be proper, so arrangements have been made," Perry replied. "How much pressure is he placing on you?"

Miss Radcliffe lowered her head, scrunching the handkerchief in her gloved fist. "He's like that with all of us," she whispered. "I knew what to expect, of course, after the way he went after poor Nelly, but I just– It makes me feel so helpless, when I know my career relies upon his good graces. I'd hoped to be able to keep him at arm's length, but he's... persistent."

That made her furious. "If you need help, you should come to us. Nothing, not even your career, is worth being pressured into a relationship you don't wish for."

"What else do I have, other than my career?" Miss

Radcliffe's smiling facade slipped, revealing a haunted edge to her eyes.

A question Perry had often asked herself. She'd forced herself to put aside any other feminine dreams to focus on her career. To forge her own path up the ladder in the Nighthawks, she'd had to be ruthless, exacting and forgo her own pleasures.

She also had no answer for Miss Radcliffe. A woman's lot was precarious in this world. "Perhaps... if you made it clear your attentions were engaged elsewhere, he might relent."

"Nobody else would dare stand up to him."

"Garrett would."

Silence bloomed. Miss Radcliffe flushed. "I-I wasn't aware that you'd noticed."

So her heart did lie in that direction. Something squeezed tight in Perry's chest, but she forced it down. A woman's safety was more important than her own insecurities.

"Or perhaps you could earn your right on the stage. If the audience loves you enough, they'll clamour your name," Perry said. "Rommell wouldn't be able to cut you from the show."

"The audience is fickle, and I'm not Nelly. She owned the crowd, you know. Flirted with all of them - men and women alike. She had this... this ability to make everyone think she belonged to them - and yet, it's only now that I realize how private she was in person. How little I knew of her."

"May I ask you a question?"

Miss Radcliffe nodded. "Of course."

"I find it curious the way you said 'Rommell went after poor Nelly'. Did he pressure her into becoming his mistress?"

Miss Radcliffe's eyes widened. "Oh, Nelly wasn't his mistress. She had a beau, I think, who sent her peonies. I caught a glimpse of the card once. It read, 'From Nick, with love', or something like that. Maybe it was Nathan? No, no it was something shorter than that."

Everything in Perry went still, as her hunting instincts rose. "It wouldn't have been James, would it?"

Miss Radcliffe shook her head. "I don't think so. I'm certain it began with 'N'. Or maybe it was Mick?" She frowned. "Nelly saw me looking, and tucked the card away, most likely to keep it quiet from Rommell. He was so focused on having her, and she put him off all these months."

Which was unusual, because Rommell had told Garrett precisely the opposite. "I was under the impression that she'd accepted his proposal."

Miss Radcliffe shook her head. "Nelly... it wasn't easy for her, but she... she managed him far better than I have. She kept pretending she'd think about it, or hinting that she enjoyed the chase, but sometimes, when he'd turn away she'd get this look in her eyes - as though he disgusted her. Rommell was desperate to have her. He kept bringing her more exotic gifts, but she'd always turn them away. It only made him more determined."

That was a very important fact. "How strange. Rommell's made it clear she was under his protection - indeed, he seemed to think that several other blue blood lord's were trying to steal her away from him."

Trying to lead her and Garrett to other potential suspects perhaps?

"Oh, he was very protective of her - or her affections, rather. And that slimy Lord Beckham's been trying to lure her to the Highcastle. Offered her a place in his troupe - and his bed, no doubt. Rommell was furious. It's like a game to them."

So Nelly wouldn't commit to Rommell, who had a direct challenge for his pursuit of her. *That* could be motive, but how did Hobbs fit into all of this? Perry's pulse quickened in excitement. All of the little bits of puzzle pieces started rearranging themselves in her head. Still not complete, but she felt like she had the edge piece of the puzzle in her hand. From there, she'd be able to start filling in the other pieces.

Was Hobbs Nelly's beau? If Nelly loved Hobbs and was seeing him privately, perhaps someone had found out? Beckham? Or Rommell? Neither of them would like discovering Nelly had a low-rate human suitor, when she'd turned both of them away.

She needed to find Garrett. Now. But first... "What was Nelly's response to Beckham? And did Rommell ever warn her away from Beckham?"

"Nelly treated Beckham the same way she treated Rommell, as if it were all a great lark, and that she might consider it, but not... not yet. And Rommell never confronted her in public, though he often sought a private audience when he came in to go over the books with Fotherham." Miss Radcliffe pursed her lips. "Although... There was an altercation here a month ago, when both Rommell and Beckham came backstage after the play. Nelly laughed it off, but she locked the door on the pair of them, and insisted on one of the stagehands seeing her to her hackney afterwards, so it must have shaken her up. The pair of them went at it, until Fotherham broke them apart, and told Beckham he was not longer welcome backstage. I never even thought to mention it. Do you think it has something to do with what happened?"

"It's something we'll consider," Perry told her. "If

anything strikes your attention as important, I'd appreciate it if you let us know. Sometimes the most random snippets of conversation can break a case."

"Of course." Miss Radcliffe nodded earnestly.

"Excuse me, ladies."

They both looked up.

Arthur Millington tipped his head to them, "Miss Radcliffe. Hope you're feeling a mite better."

Miss Radcliffe smiled. "Thank you, Arthur. I'm much recovered."

"Might I have a word, then? It's about the lighting during the third act?" Impatience made him shift under their scrutiny.

"Of course." Miss Radcliffe patted her hair into place, then handed Perry back her handkerchief. "If I think of anything I shall come directly to see you."

They hurried onto the stage, where several other actresses were gathered with Mr. Fotherham.

Perry slipped a small brass piece out of her pocket, and slipped it into her ear. Fitz, one of the other Nighthawks, had designed the aural communicators for Nighthawks who might have to work alone, and Perry and Garrett often used them. Within the range of the theatre, they'd be able to communicate, without anyone else hearing.

If Garrett had his turned on.

Perry fiddled with the frequency. She needed to find Garrett. This new information–

A scream tore through the theatre.

Perry spun toward the stage. *Miss Radcliffe!* She started sprinting, her wrist pistols spinning into her hands, as she fought her way through the sudden flurry of actresses that scattered toward the backstage and perceived safety. It was like fighting her way through a flock of startled chickens.

Gun fire barked. Perry grabbed a young woman in a ball gown and jerked her behind the nearest prop - an enormous set piece that was crafted to resemble a ballroom in some fancy Echelon manor. "Stay down!"

More screams lit the auditorium.

"Stay back, you beast!" A man yelled.

Perry crouched behind the curtains, twitching them aside in order to see. From the other side of the stage, she saw Garrett duck behind a wardrobe prop, his pistol in hand. Their eyes met and Perry nodded, feeling relief.

Miss Radcliffe was on her knees, with Arthur Millington and a couple of other stagehands forming a protective circle around her. Fotherham staggered off the stage and fell, as something pushed past him.

The huge, lumbering form roared incoherently, and drove toward the edge of the stage near where she hid. Perry stepped forward, sighting along both barrels of her wrist pistols. A hideous face swam into view, frightened eyes locking on her and yet, not seeing her. Perry's breath eased out, the world narrowing to the man's massive chest, and the sensation of her fingers easing over the triggers. At the last minute she jerked the pistols up, and he rushed past her. *Hell. That was Lovecraft—*

"Don't shoot!" she yelled, taking off after him. Leaping off the stage, she spun her pistols back into the sheaths at her wrists and started after him.

"Perry!" Garrett's voice echoed, then a curse as he realized she had no intentions of stopping.

Lovecraft lurched toward the side door, hitting it with his shoulder. Wood splintered, and he bellowed in rage, then vanished into the blinding sphere of afternoon light.

Perry winced at the brightness - her sensitive eyes preferred night - and leapt through the hole he'd created.

Her shoulder clipped a startled passer-by in a bowler hat and she spun off balance, collected herself on the base of a gas lamp, then kept going across the road as Lovecraft smashed a man off a monocycle.

Horns blared as an omnibus steered desperately around her. Perry leapt up onto the seat of a steam-carriage to the startled cry of the driver, her boot hitting the top of the carriage as she slid over the polished walnut exterior and dropped off the other side. Shock ran up her calves as she landed, and she only just managed to leap off the road as a carriage hurtled down upon her.

Ahead of her Lovecraft vanished around the corner, elbowing people out of the way. He was shockingly fast, but so too was she.

Perry went after him, ignoring the shouts behind her. He pounded through an abandoned church cemetery, long neglected, and she made up time by hurdling the iron fence, and reaching out to snatch at his sleeve as he thundered across another road.

With a snarl he threw her off, and slammed through a pair of gates into a park. A squirrel tore up the nearest tree in fright, and people looked up in shock from their picnic rugs, scrambling in a mad rush to get out of the way. There was a cricket match in progress among a flock of young schoolboys, and a gentleman in a top hat snatched a boy up under each arm, as she and Lovecraft drove straight through the middle of it.

Perry made one last-ditch effort.

"Stop!" She threw herself into a tackle, dragging him down to the grass.

A blow stung her ears, and she rolled over his shoulder in a tangle of arms and legs, until she came up against a tree.

Lovecraft staggered to his feet, and drew back his boot as if to kick her in the face.

"Lovecraft!" She held up a hand. "I'm your friend, remember? It's Perry. From Hobbs' shop!"

Recognition dawned. "Nurly," he said.

"Yes," she let out a breath of relief, not daring to move. "I'm trying to find Nelly. To help her. Why did you come to the theatre?"

"Nurly!"

"Nelly's not there, remember? She's gone away. I have to find her."

Wringing at his cap, he rocked back and forth, wide eyes frightened as he watched people running away from them. "Gone. Nurly gone. Jerm gone."

"James?" she asked. "James is gone?"

He looked panicked. Perry rolled onto her hands and knees. What was he trying to say? "I can help you," she said. "You can't find James or Nelly, can you? Is that why you came to the theatre?"

"Jerm hurt. Jerm gone."

Her breath caught in the back of her throat. "That's right. Did you see the man who hurt James?"

Tortured eyes met her own. Lovecraft tore at his cap, as though to hide behind it, but he nodded.

"Was it someone at the theatre?" she asked breathlessly. "Is that why you came there?"

Whistles screamed as the local constabulary came on the scene. Lovecraft cupped his hands over his specially-designed earmuffs, wincing. Whatever she did, she would have to do it quickly. She could see they all had pistols.

Hell and blazes. She needed time to talk to him. Lovecraft *had* witnessed Hobbs' murder - he knew who'd done it.

But if he stayed here... Where people didn't understand him...

"Go," she said, meeting his gaze, and imploring him. If they caught him, they wouldn't hesitate to shoot. Not with his appearance. People were always frightened of what they didn't understand, and Lovecraft was like a child trapped in a man's body. He wouldn't know how to appear unthreatening. "You need to run! Go! They'll hurt you! Go home! I'll find you!"

Tears wet his eyes, then the big man turned, and started running. The pair of constables bolted past her, and Perry took her time rolling to her feet, brushing the grass off.

Garrett caught up to her, grinding to a breathless halt. "Are you all right?"

Perry brushed a couple of leaves off her shoulder. "I'm fine. How is everyone at the theatre?"

"Shaken up, but not harmed. What the hell was that? Why the hell didn't you shoot?"

Perry wet her lips. "That was Lovecraft."

Garrett cut her a look. "Hobbs' adopted... project?"

"He's not a project," she said sharply.

"Did he hurt you?" He brushed grass off her arms, cupping her shoulders and turning her around to examine her. As she spun back the other way, he caught her chin, and tipped her face up, heat flaring through his blue eyes. "He hit you. You're bruised."

"It'll fade. I did tackle him, after all. He never meant to hurt me–"

"Bloody hell, Perry. It didn't look like that. You said he wasn't a threat!"

"He wasn't. At least, I didn't gain that impression. He was frightened of me–"

"I know your instincts are good," he said, in a hard tone, "but sometimes you're wrong."

"And sometimes you're a fool!" She snapped, turning back to the theatre.

He caught her arm. "You didn't see what happened, Perry! He went straight for Miss Radcliffe! Millington barely managed to push her out of the way when Lovecraft attacked. He knocked down three men, and broke another's arm. You think that's not threatening?"

"Miss Radcliffe?" she murmured, slamming to a halt. "Did he attack her?"

"Tried to."

They stared at each other.

Perry's mind raced. Was she correct? Did Lovecraft come to the theatre to get revenge on the person who'd shot Hobbs? Or had he not truly understood what she'd been trying to ask?

Was it Miss *Radcliffe*?

She too had motive. A prime new role as lead actress, and the only proof that Rommell had a hand in the disappearance, had come directly from her pretty lips.

Had that entire story earlier been something that the actress had made up? A way to cast suspicion on the lord? After all, Miss Radcliffe was an actress. Maybe the tears had been feigned?

Perry's gut twisted in doubt. If it was a lie, then the woman was one hell of an actress. Perry could have sworn those tears had been real, but how could she tell Garrett that? He already thought her hare-brained, for thinking that Lovecraft wasn't a threat to her. If she tried to tell him her suspicions about Miss Radcliffe - after all of their previous arguments - he'd no doubt think Perry was trying to stir trouble again.

"Can you track him by scent?" Garrett asked. He knew how good her senses were.

Perry hesitated - then slowly shook her head. "No. I can't smell anything."

Which was a lie, but if she were going to talk to Lovecraft then she needed to do it alone. He would be too frightened of anyone else, and she knew Garrett didn't believe her.

"Let's get back to the theatre," she said. "And see how Miss Radcliffe is faring."

And afterwards, she'd see if she could pick up the scent trail that she could sense.

THE THEATRE WAS BEDLAM.

Fear and excitement tainted the air, and it seemed the entire acting troupe had emerged from whichever little hole in the theatre belonged to them, to see what all of the fuss was about. The room was abuzz with talk that the pursuit had lost Lovecraft, as he circled back around near the theatre.

He could be anywhere nearby. Perry's fingers twitched as everyone whispered about it.

Lord Rommell was furious. "You knew this creature?" he demanded, stepping forward just enough to make her uncomfortable.

Perry found her back against the theatre wall. "I encountered him yesterday. He... he's some kind of anomaly but I don't believe he meant any harm–"

"Perhaps you shouldn't form such assumptions," Rommell replied. "Without an actual basis to your theory besides *feminine* intuition." He actually turned his back on her, focusing on Garrett. "I want a search mounted. I want this... this creature found. It's quite evident he has something to do with Nelly's disappearance, and this incompetence is not what I'm paying the Guild for. If I hadn't stepped in when I did, it would have torn poor Miss Radcliffe to pieces!"

"My lord." Garrett's lips thinned. "Of course we plan to mount a search." Those blue eyes locked on her. He'd made it clear he thought the same way Rommell did, about Lovecraft. "I'll send for reinforcements from the Guild. We'll track him down."

Perry looked away. It was bad enough for Rommell to be questioning her competence, but Garrett hadn't even made one sound of protest. He'd always backed her when people challenged her in the past, and something ached in her chest that he didn't this time.

Was she wrong? Was Lovecraft a threat to her?

She couldn't even fathom it. He seemed so childlike to her, more frightened of the world than it was of him - which was a considerable amount indeed. He had the size and capacity to do great violence, but she just couldn't see it being intentional, no matter what had occurred here earlier. He seemed to react only out of fear and pain.

Garrett offered his arm to Miss Radcliffe, who was frightfully pale. "Perhaps you'll allow me to see you home. You look like you could do with a rest?"

Perry's muscles locked tight, anticipation flaring. It would be the perfect opportunity to follow up on Lovecraft's scent alone.

"That's quite generous, Reed," Rommell broke in, "but I do believe you have work to see to. I'll escort Eliza home in my carriage." He pasted on a smile and stepped toward the actress. "Come, my dear."

"Thank you," Miss Radcliffe looked between the men. "But I don't believe I should leave, not just yet. We have a show to perform in a few hours." Sucking in a shuddery breath, she stepped away from Rommell. "I feel utterly safe with the Nighthawk's here. I'm certain they'll find the culprit - and whatever has happened to poor Nelly."

Rommell harrumphed under his breath, but he patted her gloved hand. "Such bravery, my dear. Don't you let any of this bother you. I'll summon some of my guards to the theatre to ensure your safety, and tonight shall be another triumph."

With that he was gone. Miss Radcliffe gave them both a weak smile. "I should begin to get dressed. If you'll excuse me?"

Perry watched her go. It was interesting that she recovered so quickly. Most young ladies would have suffered a fainting fit.

Or was that simply suspicion flavouring her thoughts?

Garrett let out a frustrated sigh, as most of the acting troupe broke away to prepare themselves for the play, led by Miss Radcliffe's example. It left them alone together.

"You believe me, don't you?" Perry said into the softening darkness of the stage. "I know what a threat looks like."

Garrett raked a hand through his coppery hair. He stared out over the empty theatre. "Perhaps you misconstrued Lovecraft's intentions. It happens."

Not to me. She felt numb though, all hollow inside. Garrett didn't believe her. And why should he? She had no proof. Nothing to say that the poor creature had benevolent intentions other than her intuition, which Rommell had summarily dismissed.

That made her burn with fury. Years of working cases, and men were still looking down their noses at her. "Perhaps you shouldn't believe everything Rommell says," she snapped. "Considering that he lied about Nelly being his mistress."

Garrett caught her arm as she turned to go. "What?"

"According to Miss Radcliffe, Nelly had a beau who might have been named Nick, or something similar, and that she refused Rommell's suit. Unless she's lying, I'm going to assume, with my *feminine* intuition, that Rommell is therefore a suspect. I could be wrong. Maybe I should rely on your superior instincts as a man?"

"Don't take that tone with me," he warned. "I'm not the one that doesn't trust your instincts."

"Truly?" She looked up at him. "Because it feels like you did."

They stared at each other.

"I know," he said carefully, "that I wasn't there when you encountered the creature before."

"His name is Lovecraft."

"Fine, Lovecraft." A hint of snarl coated his words. "But I saw what happened today. I saw that thing come straight at us. It threatened Miss Radcliffe, then turned on Millington and Rommell, Perry. It had murder in its eyes and you know it."

"Rommell inspires such thoughts in several of us, then. I'm having trouble keeping my knives sheathed whenever he opens his mouth."

"Rommell is of the Echelon. He could cause trouble for us very easily."

"You don't think I know that? How foolish do you consider me?"

"I'm just saying... perhaps you should let me handle him? Your emotions are involved, and while I don't like the man, I can restrain my temper around him. As for Lovecraft, don't underestimate him." He stared her in the eyes. "Promise me you'll watch your back tonight, when we mount this search."

"You're going to bring in more Nighthawks?"

He gave a clipped nod. "Unfortunately, we do need to do something to appease Rommell. He has the power to remove both of us from the case, if need be."

"Which would be very convenient if he had something to do with Nelly's disappearance," she said darkly. "Either Rommell or Miss Radcliffe is lying. I'm not certain which. They both have motive in this case."

"But why would Miss Radcliffe shoot Hobbs, if she were involved?" He said quickly.

Too quickly.

And Perry didn't have the answers to that. "I don't know. I just thought I should tell you. And why would Rommell do such a thing either? Neither of them would have come into Hobbs' sphere, unless he came to the theatre. It just seems an odd thing for either of them to lie about, but one of them must be."

A frown twisted Garrett's brow and he slid his hands into his pockets. "Something to look into then. And the Webley pistol *is* small enough to be operated by a woman."

The earlier argument hovered in the air, but at least he was taking her suspicions seriously. Perry looked away. "Perhaps you should go and see if you can organise a squad of Nighthawks?"

"And what do you intend to do?"

"I'll stay here," she said. "Make sure that the *monster* doesn't return."

"Perry–"

"I can't get into trouble that way, can I? Perhaps when

you come back you can tell me what I should do next? Since my intuition is so obviously skewed today."

He growled under his breath. "Maybe you *should* stay here and wait for me. I don't know that it's your intuition that is skewed - or perhaps your common sense - but we'll discuss that when I return."

8

Deep backstage, Perry knelt, touching her fingers to a patch of blood on the floor. The moment Garrett had left to call for reinforcements, she'd managed to pick up the scent trail in the park, and had followed it on a circuitous route back to the theatre. Now, she was no closer to finding Lovecraft, but she had the dawning suspicion that he'd returned to the scene of the crime, and was somewhere deep in the bowels of the monstrous building.

For what purpose though?

Was he frightened, or hurt or hiding? The blood certainly indicated that one of the constables had winged him.

Maybe he didn't know where to go - or had come looking for her, looking for help?

Or maybe he was here to finish the job that he'd started.

That chilled Perry's blood. What did she know about him, truly? Garrett had told her that her common sense had gone missing, and maybe he was right? Maybe she was letting her emotions make her decisions.

She still had to find him, however, before someone else did. She could prevent another incident. She just had to pray that she got to him first, before the rest of the Nighthawks arrived.

A pair of eyes gleamed in the shadows, and Perry froze as she recognised that hulking shape. Lovecraft was rocking himself in the corner, making a low, keening noise in his throat.

"Hello," she whispered. "It's me again. Perry." Her throat went dry as he stopped making that noise. She couldn't forget the way he'd attacked the group earlier. No more assumptions that he wouldn't hurt her.

Lovecraft bared his metal teeth at her in a growl, and her heart plummeted into her gut. He was truly a pathetic sight, like a scared child. How could the others not see it? The rage with which he'd assaulted Rommell and Miss Radcliffe was that of a scared young boy, not a man.

She should arrest him. Half the theatre was already up in arms, looking out for him, after the constables had said that he'd returned to this area. It wasn't safe, but if she arrested him, and they saw him... The men didn't want justice, they wanted blood.

Damn it.

Reaching out, Perry set a gentle hand on his arm. Lovecraft flinched. The scent of blood was thick here, stirring the heat inside her. Perry swallowed, and moved a little closer. "You're hurt."

Moving slowly, she peeled his arm away from his chest. Blood soaked the dirty linen shirt he wore. Someone had shot him.

Perry tugged her handkerchief out of her pocket, and pressed it to the wound. The bleeding was sluggish now, but she used his hand to hold it there, just in case. Lovecraft winced, and rested his head on her shoulder.

She'd never been good with comforting people, but it was so easy to reach out and slide a comforting hand through his hair. Perhaps because, in a way, he was like her... Not accepted, shunned, afraid of people, and the way they could mock or jeer.

"Why did you attack Miss Radcliffe?" Perry whispered.

Those guileless blue eyes were glazed with pain and exhaustion as he looked up. He looked confused.

"Miss Radcliffe," she said. "The woman on the stage. Why did you attack her?"

Lovecraft shook his head, frustration making him restless. "Nuh. Nuh. Lovecraff.. not hurr-t."

"Easy." She took his hands, and put them back on his wound. "I believe you." A hesitation. This wasn't going to be easy, but someone had to try. "You didn't try to hurt the woman on the stage, did you?"

He shook his head.

"Was it one of the men there?" There was no response, but she tried again. After all, Rommell had been standing near Miss Radcliffe – perhaps the witnesses had misconstrued Lovecraft's intended victim. "Did you see the man who hurt James?"

This time there was a nod.

Perry's breath caught. *Rommell.* It had to be Rommell. "We have to leave," she said. "It's not safe for you here. Come with me, and I'll help remove you, without being seen. I'll take you to the Guild. It will be safe there. It will–"

His eyes focused on something over her shoulder. The hairs along her neck rose as she heard a faint, shuffling footstep.

She caught just a glimpse of a man's legs behind her,

then something smashed into the back of her head with a sharp pain. Everything went dark, the sound echoing with a ringing peal through her head. The next thing she knew, there was a furious sound, men snarling as they grappled... and the imprint of the floorboards beneath her cheek.

Blinking through the pain, Perry tried to pull herself together. Her fingers refused to move, her body weighing as heavy as one of the sandbags they used for the curtains. Someone... had hit her... Lovecraft... What was happening?

Come on. Move.

All she could smell was blood. Her blood. But deep inside came that sinuous shifting as the predator within caught a teasing hint of it too. The craving stirred, washing through her vision with frightening intensity.

A shot rang out. Perry jerked, and somehow made it onto her hands and knees as something heavy hit the floor behind her. *Oh, God.* She reached for her pistol with clumsy hands, barely able to see–

Strong hands caught her up, shoving her forward behind a curtain. Her body simply wouldn't work. Couldn't fight, couldn't get her head to stop spinning–

"Meddling bitch." The word sounded so far away. "Time to see if you can swim too."

Something hard struck her across the back of the head again.

Then the floor gave way beneath her, and Perry tumbled down, down, into the cold splashy blackness of water.

9

The sound of a shot ringing out punctured the silence. Garrett slammed to the edge of the railing above the theatre, where he'd been trying to get a bird's eye view, his heart kicking into his throat. He'd returned not five minutes past, after sending a telegram to the Guild for reinforcements.

Perry?

Where the hell was she? She was supposed to wait in the theatre for him. He couldn't hear anything through the aural communicator, and she wasn't where he'd left her.

Two more shots rang out in rapid succession. "We've got him!" Someone yelled.

Garrett charged down the ladder, hitting the theatre floorboards, and running into the darkness behind the curtains. Men were pouring out of the shadows, clapping hands, laughing...

And then he realized why.

The scene was a gruesome one. One of the lighting hands - Millington, he thought - was standing over a large, fallen figure. Blood spilled from beneath Lovecraft's vacant face, and pooled beneath his massive chest. A bullet had taken him straight through the temple, and there were two more in his back.

The creature's clockwork hand twitched once - then twice - as though the clockwork mechanism hadn't realized the body attached was dead. It was somewhat eerie.

"Well done!" Rommell clapped Millington on the back, one of his feet hooked up on Lovecraft's head, like a man posing for a daguerreotype with his 'trophy'. "Hoorah, boys! The menace is dead!"

They all cheered. Garrett felt ill. And where the hell was Perry? She should have heard that, and come running.

Rommell saw him standing there, and sneered. "No thanks to you Nighthawks." He clapped Millington on the shoulder again. "Needed some real men on the case."

Garrett met Rommell's eyes, the darkness within stirring through him. Rommell's smile froze as though he sensed some of the menace, and Garrett turned away. Let them have their fun. He was here for business.

He knelt by the body. Hot red blood puddled out, soaking into the timbers, but nearby was a splash of something darker in the shadows by the back curtain. Almost a handprint of bluish-red blood, small, like a woman's hand.

No. His gaze locked on that print, and he scrambled toward it. Only those stricken by the craving virus had bluish-blood. It was what gave the blue bloods their name.

Which meant it had to have come from Rommell - or Perry.

And Rommell wasn't injured.

She'd been here. Fury and rage flooded through him, along with fear. Most of the men were still laughing, and someone had sent for the photography equipment so they could immortalise the image of Rommell standing by Love-craft, with one fist curled in the creature's hair.

Garrett shoved his way into the shadows, searching for more signs of Perry. There - another spatter of dark blood flicked up the walls. He knew the type of blood pattern. She'd been struck by something hard. Had it been Love-craft? What the hell had happened here? And where was she? Christ, he should have been here with her. Not letting her go off alone–

"What's wrong?" Miss Radcliffe was there, one hand on his sleeve, and Garrett realized the darkness within him had almost blinded him to his surroundings.

"It's Perry," he said. "She was here. She was bleeding." But she wasn't here now. Panic closed his throat until it was hard to breathe. "I don't know where she is now. She has to be hurt, but I don't know where she's gone."

Miss Radcliffe's dark eyes swam into his vision, looking worried. "Perhaps she's in one of the dressing rooms?"

He eyed that blood spatter pattern. Someone had hit her, and now she was gone. Things just weren't adding up, and he had a horrible feeling deep inside, turning his bones to lead. Instinct. The same instinct that had led Perry to believe Lovecraft wouldn't hurt her. "How could Nelly have gone missing so easily?" he murmured to himself. "No one saw her go, she just disappeared, and now Perry's vanished too, as though she was never here. How? There are only three exits from the theatre, and the place is always full of people."

"Well, there are the tunnels beneath us," Miss Radcliffe said, then her eyes widened in horror. "Oh, goodness." She slapped a hand to her mouth. "The tunnels! They were there when the new theatre was built over the last one, during the fire. They're full of water now, but I know some of the men use them to dump refuse into."

His blood was like ice in his veins. "Where?" Garrett asked hoarsely.

Miss Radcliffe swept a curtain out of the way, revealing a hidden trapdoor in the floor. "Right here."

There was a drop of dark blood on the timber floor in front of it.

10

"Perry!" Garrett yelled, his fists clenched into tight balls at his sides.

His voice echoed through the tunnels, then faded, leaving him in a ringing silence that knotted each muscle in his gut. Garrett spun, staring at the three tunnels in front of him. Water drifted slowly through them, leading to one of the underground rivers that afflicted London. Where was she?

Water sloshed about his knees as he started forward, peering into the darkness of first one tunnel, then the next. "Perry?!" *Damn you, answer me.*

His heart was starting to beat a little faster now, a little harder. She had to be down here somewhere, but why wouldn't she answer?

His mind supplied a brutal image in response to that, and Garrett shied away, shoving it deep. *No.* No, no, no. He waded further into the left tunnel, sniffing the air, desperate to find some trace of her. He'd never been a good tracker - his skills lay elsewhere - but he had to try.

A whisper of sound reverberated through the aural

communicator. Garrett stared across at the other tunnel, every muscle in his body locked tight as he cupped a hand over it, trying to pinpoint the origin of the sound. Static hissed in his ear, but that meant she had to be close, didn't it? Within two hundred feet, for the frequency to have picked up its matching communicator.

Lifting the phosphorescent glimmer ball high, he waded back into the main tunnel, and peered into the smaller access sewer across from him. Down there? There was no further sound, no scent, nothing, just the faintest of hopes.

Garrett took a step forward... and fell up to his hips in the cold, stinking water. Gritting his teeth, he surged forward, the water deepening. Its cold fingers penetrated his leather body armour, restricting the movement of his legs.

Nothing to say where she'd gone, only a certain restlessness, a need, a drive to find her. Garrett staggered through the dark, ending up chest deep in the water. The tunnel began to narrow, barely a foot above the top of the water. If she'd come this far... He hesitated.

Please. Please God, let her be alive. Words he hadn't uttered for over twenty years, when he'd been a young human lad, growing up in the rough streets of Bethnal. Blue bloods didn't believe in religion; or perhaps religion didn't believe in them. Only as demons, who deserved to die.

Garrett glanced back. Ridiculous to even think she'd come this way, through the deepening waters. Maybe he should go back? Try one of the other tunnels?

His gaze swung between both directions, but the gloom of the tunnel was calling him, and the static in his ear seemed a little louder. *Just a little further*.

Holding his breath against the frigid water, Garrett swam through the darkening depths, reaching an archway.

The water was an inch from the ceiling here. Despair filled him.

"Perry!" he called again, the desperate echoes of his voice ringing in the tunnels. *Where the hell are you?*

He turned to swim back the way he'd come, but something caught his eye through the archway. Garrett gulped a mouthful of filthy water as he swung the glimmer ball that way desperately, clutching at the arch as he gagged on the water.

Nothing.

Still, his heart thundered in his ears. He ducked under the arch and kicked forward, coming up into a larger cavern. The glimmer light stained the world green and...

There. Something shiny-slick in the water.

Leather.

His heart leapt into his throat, and he splashed forward, his feet finding purchase as he half-strode, half-swam. There was definitely something in the water. Thank God.

"Perry?"

Grabbing hold, he dragged her into his arms. Perry was heavier than he'd anticipated, a solid weight in his arms that surprised him. Her pale, frigid face surfaced out of the water, lips painted an eerie blue.

"Perry?" he whispered.

Not a sign of recognition. Not a sound.

She wasn't breathing.

Everything in him went cold.

11

on't you dare die on me.

D Garrett hauled Perry into his arms, kicking out for the nearby ledge. He dragged her out of the water, and let her fall onto the cold stone, jerking at her coat, and the tight silver buckles on her armoured corset. She had to breathe. Had to. He wouldn't accept any other possibility.

Her head lolled bonelessly to the side as he resorted to using his knife, cutting the tight, wet leather corset, and tearing its edges apart with desperate hands. "Come on," he snapped, stroking the wet hair off her pale face as he rolled her to the side, and thumped her hard in the centre of the back, her wet undershirt clinging to her skin.

Water spilled from Perry's mouth. Not enough though. Garrett tried again and again, on her side, on her back, using the pressure of his hands to shove at her abdomen. Her head was bleeding, and he felt the pulpy softness at the base of her skull that indicated where she'd been hit from behind.

"You stubborn bitch." Heat warmed the back of his eyes

as he cupped her face in his palms, leaning over her. He could feel each tick of the minutes slowly thudding by, the weight of time pressing down on him. How long had she been in the water? His mind raced. Ten minutes? She'd been missing for a good twenty.

Garrett leaned forward, pressing his lips against her cold ones, and breathing into her mouth. He'd seen it done once before, when a young lass tumbled into the Thames when he'd been a boy.

The girl hadn't survived.

But Perry wasn't human. The only ways to truly kill a blue blood were by decapitation or removing the heart. The craving virus could heal *anything*.

Couldn't it?

Garrett breathed for her again and again. She was so cold, like ice. Despair broke over him. "Come on. I'm going to tan your hide when you're breathing again." He couldn't stand the cold of her, using his hands to rub her chest and arms, pausing just long enough to force air into her mouth. "Come on."

A sudden cough spilled water into his face. Garrett jerked back in shock as her eyes sprung wide, and she choked on the water in her mouth and lungs. He shoved her onto the side, thumping her hard in the middle of the back as water vomited from her mouth in hideous retching noises.

"Perry. Oh, God, Perry." He dragged her into his arms as the sound of a breath tore through her throat; the most painful - and wonderful - sound he'd ever heard. A hand caught at his, a terrified cry ripping through her raw throat as her body bowed.

He rocked her against his chest. "I've got you. You're safe. I've got you."

Fingers curled in the wet lapels of his coat. Another rasping breath of sound made his chest tighten... but at least she was breathing again.

Garrett pressed his cold lips against her forehead, screwing his eyes closed. He didn't want to let her go, but reason demanded that he keep them moving, and get some blood into her. She'd be weakened now, as the craving virus sought to heal her scarred lungs.

Cutting his wrist, he held it to her lips. Perry's eyes darkened as the hunger caught hold, but he didn't like how unfocused they were.

"Drink," he encouraged, holding her mouth to his wrist.

Perry's mouth locked over his skin, and the hunger within her flared to life. The hot bite of her saliva flooded the wound, and Garrett let out a breath of relief as she started drinking.

Someone had shoved her down that trapdoor into the water. Garrett rocked her gently in his arms as she collapsed back against him. Her eyelashes fluttered, and she was sated and sleepy now, his blood already flushing through her system. She'd heal.

But someone else wouldn't. Garrett was going to tear the bastard who'd done this limb from limb.

As soon as Perry woke up and told him who it was.

Curling her in his arms, Garrett turned and waded to his feet. He passed the main tunnel, the gleam of the discarded glimmer ball floating beneath the eerie darkness of the waters. Something pale ghosted beneath the surface, and Garrett caught a glimpse of pallid flesh. *What the hell?* He paused and nudged the glimmer ball he'd dropped closer to the shape.

A bloated set of fingers floated into view.

12

"I'm sorry to ask this," Garrett murmured, pushing open the door to the autopsy room at the Guild headquarters. "But we need a positive identification, and in the absence of Nelly's familial background, it has to be someone she worked with."

Miss Radcliffe swallowed, looking pale. "Of course."

Doctor Gibson looked up from his file, then gestured the actress toward the autopsy table. "There is some mild decomposition," he murmured, lifting back the sheet a couple of inches. "It's not very pleasant to look at. Please let us know if you're feeling unwell."

One glimpse. That was all it took.

Miss Radcliffe's eyes filled with tears, and she managed a brief nod, before turning away to cup her hands over her face. Garrett gestured for Doctor Gibson to drag the sheet up over the dead woman's face, and slid a hand over Miss Radcliffe's shoulder.

"Is it Nelly?" he asked, though he was certain. What other woman would have only one leg?

"Y-yes."

Seeing her distress, Garrett ushered her out into the corridor, away from the stale scent of formaldehyde and death. Miss Radcliffe burst into a storm of weeping, and he gently rubbed her between the shoulder blades.

"I'm sorry," she hiccupped, cleaning her face with the handkerchief he offered.

"Don't be. You've had a horrific day, Eliza, and this is only another nightmare to add to it. Thank you for your help. It's very important to the case."

"I truly thought she was going to come home to the theatre," Miss Radcliffe whispered. "I kept believing it was just a few more days until she was back, and now here she is... and she's been there all along and none of us even knew and–"

"We'll take care of it," he promised, rubbing her upper arms.

"Was it... deliberate?"

Garrett's lips thinned and he nodded. After what had happened to Perry he had a good idea of how poor Nelly had met her end. Doctor Gibson needed to inspect her lungs, but the obtrusion on the back of her head indicated she'd been struck with something at some stage, then she'd probably drowned, slipping beneath those dark waters without even a struggle.

So he had the means of her murder now, but not the why of it. Or the who.

Rommell? Or Beckham?

No. No, it had to be someone who knew the theatre well enough to know the water-filled tunnels were below. The idea of Rommell having knowledge of an illicit means to dump refuse was ludicrous.

The assault had happened in Nelly's dressing room, as evidenced by the blood spatter. Then the murderer had somehow removed her without anybody seeing, and dumped her down the chute without so much as a by-your-leave.

"That trapdoor you showed me," he said. "Is that the only access to the tunnels from within the theatre itself?" He knew there were other exits - he'd removed Perry through a small sewer grate in the nearby streets.

Miss Radcliffe nodded. "As far as I'm aware of. It's not something one pays a great deal of attention to. You would have to ask the stagehands, or the cleaning staff."

He certainly intended to ask. Now that they had Nelly's body, and knew what had become of her, he had a good solid lead.

Seeing Miss Radcliffe into a steam-cab with a few more questions, he found his steps heading toward the infirmary. The worst was over. Garrett knew that, but from the knot in his guts, his body didn't.

Garrett checked on Perry for the fourteenth time that day, easing the infirmary door open and just staring. Perry lay curled on her side, the short shock of silky dark strands darkening the pillow, and the half circle of her lashes fluttering uneasily against her pale cheeks.

The soft sound of her breathing was the only thing that grounded him.

She was tall for a woman; lean and strong, but here in the infirmary she looked frighteningly pale, and so small beneath the sheets. Garrett crossed the room on cat-silent feet. He didn't know how long he stood there, until Doctor Gibson made a sound of disapproval behind him, clearing his throat. Garrett spun, holding up his hands in surrender as the good doctor jerked a thumb toward the door.

Gibson mainly handled autopsies, but in the event of a serious injury, he often saw to the Nighthawks themselves. It was rare that a blue blood couldn't heal from an injury, though occasionally Gibson's dab hand with a needle sped the process up. The craving virus took care of the rest.

The moment the door was closed, Gibson sighed. "Christ, lad. I told you to let her be. She needs rest and blood, and she'll be hale in no time."

Garrett couldn't quite explain the obsessive need to check on her. He'd spent most of the day pacing the hallway, fighting the horrible certainty that she'd stopped breathing again.

He still didn't know what had drawn him down that tunnel. Instinct? Some sound or scent that his mind hadn't quite recognised? What if he'd turned around, and gone back? He couldn't stop thinking about it.

Gibson saw it on his face. "Fine, lad. Just don't wake her up when you check on her."

"I won't," Garrett promised, relief flooding through him as he turned to stalk through near-silent corridors.

He left Perry alone, pacing into the depths of the guild. Smoke curled through his nostrils, tainted with chemical. Fitz's dungeon. Garrett strode past, then paused, rapping sharply on the door.

It jerked open, and Fitz blinked through a pair of magnifying goggles at the sight of him. "Garrett. Come in."

Feeling restless, he paced in front of the fire, rubbing at the back of his neck. "I need you to do something for me."

The room was a mess of benches, all of them smothered in an assortment of gears and metalwork, with fine tools hanging from hooks on the walls. "Of course. What is it?"

Garrett surveyed the gleaming glass eye that stared back at him from some sort of mechanical creature the young man was creating. He took a deep breath. "I need you to create a device for me, a method of tracking a person. It needs to be small and subtle, so that she's not aware of being traced."

"A case?" Fitz asked dryly, "or is this some new concept of courting a woman that I've not heard of?"

Of course he wouldn't have heard. Down here in the bowels of the guild, Fitz rarely came up for air - let alone conversation. The young blue blood was so absorbed in his mechanics that he rarely mingled with others.

"Neither. I'm going to put it on Perry."

Fitz winced. "Good luck with that."

Garrett privately agreed. She'd have his guts for garters. No doubt she'd think it some insane notion that he didn't respect her skills.

How to tell her that there was another reason entirely? That it would allow him to work with her again, without sending him into a rousing panic that something might happen to her again?

He couldn't lose her. He'd never precisely thought of it in terms of such, but their friendship was one of the things he valued most in the world.

"Just create something for me," Garrett said. "I'll do the rest."

Somehow he'd discover a way to put a tracking device on her.

Then he'd never lose her again.

THE SUMMONS CAME THAT EVENING.

Garrett climbed the stairs to the second floor where Lynch's study and personal rooms were, his heart as heavy as his feet. Taking a deep breath, he rapped his knuckles on the door.

"Come in."

Fire crackled in the grate, and Lynch's focus was entirely on the case file in front of him as he made notations. Garrett waited in front of the desk, his hands clasped behind him.

Lynch finished what he was doing, and put his spring-pen aside, leaning back in his chair. He crossed his hands over his middle. "So what happened?"

"I assumed you saw the briefing note?"

"Yes, but I'm asking *you*. There are some inconsistencies that I'm not quite certain how to interpret."

Hell and damnation. Garrett turned aside, crossing to the window to look out. He knew exactly what his superior was asking of him, and he hated to know that he'd let both Lynch and Perry down in this circumstance. "I made a mistake." One hell of a mistake. His fingers curled into a fist. "I accept full responsibility for what happened."

"Which was?"

Shaking his fist, Garrett slowly uncurled it, and rested his fingers on the windowsill. "Perry and I... There was an argument between us during the initial questioning on the day Miss Tate disappeared. Then another argument... and another. It just kept escalating. I let my anger with her direct my actions, and when it came to that day at the theatre, I... I cast doubt on her intuition and we argued again." The weight of it was like a mountain, sitting heavily on his shoulders. "I let her remain behind alone, when I shouldn't have. I let..." And this was the hardest admission of all. "I let an attraction I felt for a witness compromise my case, and my duty toward my partner."

The only thing that broke the silence was Lynch's sigh, a sound so filled with disappointment that Garrett had to swallow the furious lump in his throat. Why the hell had he been so bloody stupid? Arrogance and petty anger had nearly cost him his partner's life.

"I've never had this problem with either of you. You always work exceptionally well together. Why now? What drove this argument? Your personal involvement with the witness?"

"At first." The words came spilling out of him, the story grudging, but he had made the mistake. It was his duty to rectify the situation. With every word, Garrett felt like he was looking at the situation again, and seeing it in a new light. Wondering why the hell certain things he'd said had seemed to infuriate Perry. Even looking back now, he still couldn't work it out.

By the time he'd finished, some of the weight had shifted from his shoulders. Not all of it, but some. "I made a monumental mistake, and Perry nearly paid for it. I almost got her killed." Garrett's voice roughened. "It will never happen again. Never."

Lynch looked thoughtful. "That explains your part in it, but the idea behind a partnership is that there are two people involved. From what I understand, Perry let pride – or God knows what – drive her to search for a potentially dangerous witness on her own. She should have waited for you, regardless of an argument. Do you think that something is bothering her? Something outside the case?"

"I don't know," Garrett admitted, and it bothered him. The whole damned mess bothered him. "We've been... dancing around each other a little." Not working together at all.

"It seems out of character for her." Lynch frowned. He'd been making notes the entire time Garrett had been speaking, which was utterly humiliating.

Garrett knew Lynch kept files on all of his Nighthawks,

but for this to be written up...He didn't say anything however. It was only pride again, eating at him. He'd earned whatever scorn Lynch could cast his way.

"She's usually more careful than this."

"Sometimes... she takes risks when her gender is challenged," Garrett said carefully. "And Rommell was getting under her skin. I– I didn't support her when Rommell accused her of making a foolish decision, because she's a female. Perhaps she felt she had something to prove."

"Hmm." Lynch drummed his finger on the desk. "Do you think she's a risk to herself in the field?"

In the field...? "Sir, she's barely–"

"She'll heal." Lynch looked up from beneath hooded eyelids. "But in the meantime, I certainly don't intend to see my two best Nighthawks on scullery duty."

"That's it? You're not punishing us?"

"Do I need to offer punishment?" Lynch quirked a brow. "Or are you simply looking for something to absolve you of your guilt?"

"Sir, I–"

"Finish the case," Lynch cut him off, uncapping his pen. He dragged open another case file and began perusing it. "I shall give Perry another day to recover – Doctor Gibson informs me that the craving virus has healed all of her wounds, and that she'll be well in no time. In the meantime, you will work with Byrnes. Once Perry is on her feet, she'll rotate in."

"I'd rather she didn't," Garrett said bluntly. "Let me and Byrnes handle it."

"The answer to that is no. I don't give a damn what the argument between you pertains to. You will, however, discover a means to deal with it between the pair of you. You will work with her, Garrett, and you will do everything in your power to keep her safe, and to solve this murder. I will expect nothing less of you."

"Yes, sir."

Lynch's dark head lowered again. "Dismissed."

DAWN SPILLED through the thin metal slats that covered the window. Someone had opened them. Perry winced, dragging the sheet up over her aching head, and burrowing into the warm mattress beneath her.

A hand snuck beneath the blankets, and tickled her bare foot. Perry jerked upright, her knees drawn in against her chest.

"No time for that," Garrett said. "You've been asleep for two days."

Finding herself wearing little more than an old nightshirt someone had dressed her in - hopefully not Garrett! - she dragged the blankets around her chin. "What are you doing in here?"

Garrett lounged back onto her bed, sprawling on his elbows. "I wanted to see how you were."

She swallowed, feeling the faint echo of rawness in her throat. "Why? What–" Looking around, brought her the realization that she was in the Guild. The last thing she could recall was falling through the trapdoor into the icy cage of water. Feeling it crawl up her body, the pressure of it tight on her lungs, leaving no room, no air for her, no–

Garrett caught her hand, his jaw set in a firm line as he avoided her gaze. "Aye, I know."

"How did I get here?"

"I found you." The expression on his face was devoid of emotion, but his fingers tightened on hers, and all of a sudden, something darkened in his eyes, as if he saw something she didn't. Or relived it, perhaps. "You weren't breathing."

Of course not. She remembered the water washing through her lungs, burying her under it until there was no air... Garrett's grip bought her back into the world.

"You're safe now," he said hoarsely. "And if you ever bloody go off by yourself again, I'll tan your hide. You went after Lovecraft, didn't you?"

Everything came rushing back. Perry tipped her chin up. "I had a job to do."

"*We* had a job to do. That doesn't mean–"

"You were busy." She threw aside the blankets. "And despite what you thought, I was right. Lovecraft was the key to it - he saw the man who shot Hobbs. Perhaps you should have listened to me - instead of hurrying to placate that blue blood leech - and then none of this would have happened."

There was a decanter of blood on the small table by the bed. Perry's hand shook as she forced herself to pour a glass of it. *Decorum*. Still, as it wet her lips, she drank in greedy gulps. Finally the lingering silence caught her attention.

Garrett looked as though she'd kicked him in the cods. His entire face had paled, dark shadows ringing his eyes. For the first time she noticed the strain there. Had he even slept? He looked dreadful. Garrett never looked anything short of impeccable, but now she saw that his coppery hair was ruffled, as though he'd run both hands through it, and his clothes were rumpled so severely that it looked like he'd slept in them.

And then she realized what she'd said to him. Careless, spiteful words. She might as well have used her knife. "Garrett–"

"No. You're right. You nearly died, and it's my fault. You

think I don't know that? You think I haven't played out every possible scenario for the past two days, wondering what might have happened if I didn't turn down that tunnel, where I found you?" His voice hardened. "I'm sorry. God, I'm so sorry, Perry."

The abject misery in his expression stole her breath, and when she reached out, he clasped her hand in his, and cupped it against his face, his lashes curtaining his eyes. The roughened stubble along his jaw grazed her palm, and Perry brought her other hand up to cradle his cheek.

"I shouldn't have gone after Lovecraft by myself," she whispered. "I should have waited for you. This is as much my fault as yours."

"I wish I could believe that."

He looked up, and the choking blue of those eyes made her heart ache in her chest. Guilt wielded a heavy lash. Perry's shoulders softened, "I'm sorry too."

Another moment of hesitation, of doubt, and then he dragged her into his arms, the scent of his clothes enveloping her, and her face tucked tight against his throat. The tight crush of his grip drove the breath from her body, and Perry realized her breasts were pressed hard against his chest. A part of her wanted to stay there, just as she knew that she shouldn't. Longing ached within her, that horrible yearning she was trying not to let herself feel. Perry closed her eyes and drank in the sensation. *Just this once.*

And only once, would it be. With a sigh, she pushed at him, but his strong arms only tightened.

"Please," Garrett whispered. "Just let me hold you."

Perry gave in, her entire body relaxing into his grip. His cool breath stirred against her cheek, one of his hands sliding down the centre of her back, tracing the indentations of her spine. His breath eased from his body in one long exhalation, and he turned his face into the curve of her throat. The intimacy of the moment was uncomfortable. How she'd longed for something like this – for him to say those words, or for him to hold her. If he ever guessed... The thought was like a wet drip of icy water down her spine, and she cleared her throat. "Garrett? This is indecent. I'm only wearing a nightshirt."

"Christ, I've seen you in your unmentionables before - that time when I didn't realize you were getting changed and barged into your room. It's not as though I think of you as a woman, Perry."

Her heart broke. With a stiff nod, Perry turned away, and poured herself another glass of blood. Of course, he didn't care. What did it matter if he saw her bare legs? It wasn't as though she were female in his eyes. Perry knew that. She'd worked hard to never let him know what beat in her chest, or how much it hurt every time she saw him with another woman.

Just once, she'd like to let him know she had needs and desires too. To give into the yearning that burned in her heart... To kiss him...

Instead, she drained the glass. Then another. She couldn't risk it. What would she do if he laughed at her? Or worse, looked at her with a guilty expression as he tried to carefully explain that he didn't feel the same way.

Never.

She could never tell him. Just bury it deep, where it didn't hurt anymore - or if it did, she could pretend that it didn't.

Garrett, of course, was oblivious. "Did you see who hit you?"

The events were hazy, and Perry shook her head.

That made him sigh, but he reached inside his coat, and

removed a long narrow box, tied with pretty ribbon. "I have something for you."

"What is it?"

"It's a present," he said. "People give them to each other. Usually the purpose of the idea is to–"

Perry tugged the ribbon open.

"Oh." Her breath caught. "It's–" *Exquisite.* She lifted the sheathed dirk out of the tissue paper and drew the blade. It was eight inches long and stiletto-thin. The kind of weapon meant to slip between a pair of ribs, rather than a slashing blade. Perry rolled it over her fingers, learning the weight and balance of it.

Garrett took it from her, sheathing the blade. "I meant to keep it until your birthday, but it seemed..." He shrugged. "Here, it's made to be sheathed inside your corset, so that you can keep it hidden." He showed her the way the sheathe had been specifically designed for the purpose. Perry couldn't take her eyes off his face, but he didn't notice.

"Thank you," she said. "It's perfect. It's the most beautiful present anyone has ever given me."

That earned a smile. "Well," he drawled. "I thought about ribbons and perfume and fripperies, but then I saw this and realized it's the perfect accessory for the lady who likes to kill things. But in all seriousness..." Those blue eyes lost their focus again, the smile fading. "It will help protect you, Perry, when I'm not there to do it. Promise me you'll keep it on you at all times."

The vulnerability in his gaze made her skin itch. "I think you hit *your* head," she said, trying for lightness. "You seem to have mistaken me for some sort of damsel in distress."

"I don't mistake you for anything you're not," he countered. "But even the most trained professionals can become vulnerable, and I won't ever allow anything to happen to you again."

"You can't protect me from the world."

"I can try." Gruff words. He glanced away, as if holding her gaze was too much for him at the moment.

Perry looked away too, fingers toying with the edge of the knife. *What to say to that?* The conversation had veered rather uncomfortably into areas she wasn't certain she liked. It only gave her treacherous heart hope, when she knew there was none.

Clearing her throat, she said: "So what have I missed? I assume you've been working on finding Miss Tate?"

That made his lips thin. "Actually, we found her..." He filled in the details of the last two days – and how he'd found poor Nelly's body, discarded in the water with her.

"A blow to the head, according to Gibson, in much the same manner as yours." Garrett's expression darkened, and she knew he was thinking of that moment again. "Byrnes and I have been keeping an eye on Miss Radcliffe, though things at the theatre seem to have settled since Lovecraft's death. We're not certain if he's the one who assaulted her in the alley that day, or someone else. They're starting their run again tomorrow night, so the theatre's been mostly closed. It's given Byrnes and I time to examine it."

"Nothing new?"

"Only one thing. We've found a dressing room trunk near the chute, shoved out of the way with some props. There's blood in it. I need Eliza to look at it, and see if the trunk belonged to Nelly. It's very similar in design to another in Nelly's dressing room, and I was wondering whether that's how her body was removed to the chute without anybody noticing. She might have been unconscious inside it."

"And... Lovecraft? It was quick?"

"Immediate." Garrett hesitated. "I know you felt a sense of responsibility for him, but–"

"He had no one else," she replied, her gaze lowering, and her arms hugging tight around her abdomen. *I know what that feels like. To be alone without any hope in the world, and only enemies everywhere you looked...*

At least she'd found the Nighthawks. Lovecraft had never had an opportunity like that, and she felt a guilty little squeeze in her chest. Could she have done more? Heard her attacker coming, perhaps? Or if she hadn't been so focused on Lovecraft, or distracted...

Garrett caught her chin. His expression was firm. "He was with someone who cared for him when he died, Perry. That's the least that anyone can ask for. You are not to blame for this. You didn't shoot him, did you?"

"Who did?" Her memories of the event were so damned hazy...

"Arthur Millington."

"The stagehand?"

He nodded. "Rommell's crowing about it as though he held the pistol himself."

That made no sense. "Millington..." His face swam to mind as the man who'd taken Miss Radcliffe away to see to the lighting. "Why would he have any cause to attack me?"

"He wouldn't, but there were three bullets that hit Lovecraft. The one through the chest was a .442 - the same bullet as the one that killed Hobbs. The other two shots were fired from a different pistol."

"So Millington shot Lovecraft twice, just before the murderer added his own bullet?"

"The results came through this morning, so I haven't had

a chance to question Millington about who else was accompanying him."

"It could be Rommell," she mused, with a small frown. "He was there too, you said."

"My money's on Rommell, though I'm not certain his lordship would carry a Webley - he's the sort to purchase a more expensive weapon, and we still don't have motive for Hobbs' murder."

"Yes, we do," she snorted. "Nelly's easy - she refused to be his mistress, and it's clear he's jealous of his possessions. Maybe he discovered that Hobbs was sending Nelly roses? Maybe he realized they were lovers?"

"We don't know that they were lovers," he said. "We don't have any proof. This is all guesswork, Perry, and if it is Rommell, we need cold, hard facts, or the courts will eat us alive. The Echelon won't like knowing that one of their own is involved in this."

"That's true."

He rubbed at his mouth. "We need to find the link between Nelly and Hobbs."

"Has Fitz had any luck with the coded diaries in Hobbs' storeroom?"

"Yes. They're mostly files on the mech enhancements he'd performed in the last few years. There's no reference to Nelly, dash it all, but it was a good thought. I'm hoping we'll be able to get a lead tomorrow."

"We?"

"Doctor Gibson needs to clear you for duty." There was a faint hesitation from him. "Lynch intends for us to work together to finish the case. I asked if I could work with Byrnes until it was finished but–"

"*What?*"

"It made sense. Not only are you injured, but you and I

have several things we need to discuss. I'd prefer to work these matters out when we have time, not in the middle of a potentially dangerous case."

The words sounded reasonable, but all she could hear was the sound of rushing thunder in her ears. "Don't you dare push me off this case."

"Christ," he snapped, his roughened accent emerging in the heat of his temper. "This ain't..." He closed his eyes and took a breath. "This has nothing to do with your worth, Perry. This entire case has been a mess from the start, and I don't even bloody know what we're arguing about!"

They glared at each other. Perry turned away first. She wasn't entirely certain why she was so angry with him.

Or perhaps she knew exactly why.

I don't even bloody know what we're arguing about... And he didn't. Garrett was completely oblivious to the way she felt about him.

She'd been oblivious.

Perry had always known he carried on affairs, but Garrett was discreet and usually conducted them outside guild matters. Usually she only realized what was going on when she smelt a hint of perfume on his skin. She'd never been present during the start of the flirtation, and it had rocked her to see him smiling and flirting with Miss Radcliffe, whom he obviously found attractive.

And why wouldn't he? The young actress was beautiful, gracious, and brave. Everything that a young lady should be, and everything that Perry wasn't. Perhaps that was the true problem? Miss Radcliffe was so perfect - the kind of young woman that Perry had once wished she could be, before realizing that no matter how hard she forced herself, she would never fit that mold.

She'd accused him of letting his emotions and flirtations

interfere with their work, when she'd compromised it far
more severely.

This was all her fault.

"Perry, are you all right?" The floorboards creaked as he
took a step toward her. "I didn't mean to say I didn't wish to
work with you. I didn't mean—"

"I know you didn't." She'd made a right royal muck of
things. "I shouldn't have made you feel like you'd compromised your professionalism. You didn't. It was only—"

"No, you were right. I was attracted to Miss Radcliffe, and
I couldn't see it, so don't apologise for that." Garrett stepped
into her vision, taking her by the upper arms. This time his
grip was firm, his expression more confident than it had
been before. "Apology accepted?"

"Apology accepted," she repeated. "Back to Nelly's apartment tomorrow?" she asked, forcing her voice to lighten, as
though nothing had ever occurred between them.

He nodded. "I'll try and track Millington down today
with Byrnes, and see if he has any answers. You just rest.
Tomorrow we'll see if we can find anything at Nelly's that we
missed in the first sweep, now we know what to look for."

Determination filled her. Cases could often be slow, but
Perry needed to find some answers now, with three people
dead. Poor Lovecraft, he'd never stood a chance...

I'll find them, she promised Lovecraft silently. *And I'll
make them pay for what they did to the pair of us, for what they
did to Nelly and Hobbs...*

The darkness of the hunger surfaced within her at the
thought.

13

Millington was at The Cap and Thistle, in Holborn, with several fellows who met for darts each Sunday. The Cap and Thistle was an old pub, with diamond-shaped windowpanes, and mahogany paneling inside. It stunk of smoke and beer, and laughter rocked its small confines.

Garrett strode in and located his target, throwing darts in the corner.

"That him?" Byrnes asked, at his side.

"Aye."

Millington swilled a mugful of beer, laughing at something someone had said. It had taken three hours to track him down - both by rumor of his habits on his day off, and his scent trail. Byrnes was almost as good at tracking as Perry was.

Millington saw them enter over the rim of his mug, and choked a little on his beer. Garrett tipped his chin, indicating he wanted a word, and Millington handed the pair of darts in his hand to someone else.

"Christ," the man muttered. "Ain't you fellows finished

up, yet? Thought we got him."

Garrett's smile was tight. "We're not entirely certain Lovecraft had anything to do with Nelly Tate's murder, but what I want to speak to you about is what occurred when you shot him. Specifically, if there was another individual in the area when you arrived on scene."

Millington grumbled under his breath as he dragged out a barstool, the whites of his eyes flashing as he eyed the dartboard longingly. "I can't bloody remember. Were about a dozen of us, all told, and it all happening at once..."

"And the pistol you were carrying at the time?" Byrnes asked.

"A Colt 1862 Trapper. Why?"

A .36 caliber. "No reason."

Garrett grilled him for the next half hour but the story didn't change. Millington seemed uninterested.

"Bloody hell, we got him, didn't he?" A sneer curled his lip. "Took care o' matters when you lot couldn't. You ain't got any proof that clockwork menace did it? Hell, you only had to look at him!"

"In the Nighthawks, we prefer facts."

"Attacked Miss Radcliffe, he did!"

"Did he?" Garrett murmured, then deliberately set out to fish for information. "I was under the impression that she simply got in his way."

Millington's eyes narrowed. "Saw it with me own eyes. You ask Lord Rommell! He were there, too."

"Yes, we're aware that Rommell was standing there. Makes us all kinds of curious." Byrnes cut him an enigmatic smile that could have meant anything.

"Rommell's a good man," Millington blustered. "Took care of matters when you lot didn't." He drained the dregs of his beer, and slammed the mug down. "I've had enough of this. The monster's dead. Case is solved. You ought to move on."

"The problem is, that whoever the other person is that shot Lovecraft, is also responsible for assaulting my partner, Perry." Garrett bared his teeth in a smile. "I'm afraid I'm not just going to let that sit."

Millington paled at the threat. "The lass as dresses like a man?"

"Yes." Garrett stood, shrugging back into his leather coat. "I'm fairly certain that when she wakes up, she'll be able to point us in the right direction. I was hoping you might have had an idea, but I suppose we'll just have to wait for Perry."

"INTERESTING TACTIC THERE," Byrnes commented as they strode along the footpath. "I thought Perry was awake."

"She is," Garrett replied.

"You suspect something?"

"Millington?" His brows shot up. "I'm not certain. He was very defensive."

"Covering for someone?"

"Possibly. Either that, or he doesn't like us very much."

"If he does know who did it, then that somebody just received fair warning," Byrnes pointed out.

Garrett felt a tight smile stretch over his face. "Good. I want them to be warned. I want them on edge about what Perry might know. So far we've got very little. Maybe this will push the murderer into revealing his hand."

Byrnes laughed under his breath, an evil sound. "That sounds like something I would have done." He looked impressed and clapped a hand on Garrett's shoulder. "Perhaps you're not such a hopeless case, after all."

14

Nelly's flat was near Portman Square. It was a cosy little one-bedroom flat, and far more ordinary than Perry had expected. Nelly's dressing room at the Veil was that of a theatre starlet; her home belonged to an entirely different woman indeed. The quilt on the bed was handmade, and much mended - as though it had been a treasured item - and dozens of poetry books and plays lay scattered around the sofas that sprawled through the main room.

Morning light streamed through the lacy curtains. Perry ransacked the room, taking less care this time to disturb matters. Poor Nelly was dead - she wouldn't care - and they needed to find information. Time was ticking out on them. Rommell had withdrawn the private commission that morning, considering the case to be solved.

Lynch had given them two days to find something, or he was going to have to pull them from the case, and put them on something else.

"Over my dead body," Garrett had muttered, as they left to

search the flat. Tension rode his hard frame, and it was clear he was still taking her assault personally.

For the first time in days, they were working as one, the way they always had. It was both a relief and a frustration - like poking at a sore tooth. The argument had fallen behind them, but she still felt as though it chafed deep inside her. Her own raw feelings, threatening to dislodge this tentative peace.

She *had* to keep them hidden away.

"Found anything?" Garrett asked, poking his head into the bedroom.

"Nothing." She tossed aside a pair of pillows, running her hands under the mattress. "Anything from the neighbours?"

"We're in luck. Since our last visit, the lady next door asked her granddaughter if she'd seen anyone calling. The granddaughter was cleaning her grandmother's windows one day when she said she saw Nelly meet a young man across the street. She'd never seen him before, but she noted that he handed Nelly a posy of *peonies*," he emphasized the word with a waggle of his eyebrows, "and that she laughed, and tucked her arm in his, before they hopped on the omnibus. This was about three weeks ago."

"I wonder why Nelly was so secretive?" Perry mused. "Why meet him at the park? She's an actress, so it's not as though she has any great reputation to protect - and I mean that with all due respect."

"Interesting thought... You're right. She's acting as though she has something to hide."

"But from whom?" Something else occurred. "The grand-daughter said he looked young? Hobbs was middle-aged. How old is the granddaughter?"

"Almost twenty, perhaps."

"She's not going to think Hobbs was young. Any other description?"

"He was wearing a cap, so she couldn't see his hair. Tall, somewhat lanky, wearing a tweed suit. It was too far away to get a good view, but she definitely recalls the incident. Remembers thinking to herself how lovely it was that Nelly had a beau. Nelly's always been good to her grandmother, you see. Keeps an eye out."

And Miss Radcliffe had mentioned the card attached to the flowers Nelly had received, from someone named Nick or Mick, or something similar. What if they'd been wrong all along? What if Nelly *had* been seeing someone in secret? Someone they didn't yet know about? "Let's keep searching then."

Together, they turned toward the living areas. Several long fruitless minutes passed.

A typeset play with dog-eared pages rested on the edge of the chair by the window, as if Nelly had been going through it the day before she disappeared. Little hand-written notes filled the margins. Perry had glanced at it before, and dismissed it after a brief glimpse, but now she flipped through it.

'Oh, Ned, I love this line. It's brilliant! And so naughty.'

She was about to put the play down, when a name caught her eye.

'You wicked man! I know exactly who this Edward Mayhue character is based on. It's James to a T! All puffed up importance, and I-know-what's-best! I wonder if Clarissa is going to turn out to be his secret sister, hmm?'

Perry paused, her thumb ruffling the corners as she flicked through the pages. Another little scrawl caught her eye.

'And now Clarissa meets the stable hand? I'm practically

dying of laughter here. It's brilliant! I wonder if James will even recognise it all when he sees it on stage? I wonder if Rommell will? Please tell me his pompous lordship meets a bad end instead of marrying poor Clarissa?'

Perry flipped back to the start, and began reading. It seemed to be a comedy, in which the heroine, Clarissa Donovan, was pursued by the odious Lord Carthark, much to the disgust of her half-brother, Edward. Clarissa meanwhile, was in love with her brother's stable hand, right beneath the noses of both Edward and Lord Carthark.

The humour was considerably bawdy, and some of Clarissa's antics made her eyebrows lift. It was the type of play Garrett would have loved.

"What have you got there?" he asked, noticing her absorption.

"I'm not entirely certain. I think it's telling us something. I think Nelly did have a beau - this Ned. Come look!" She flipped back to the note about James. "I don't think James was her beau, after all. I think he's her brother."

It was the closest they'd come to finding any sort of background on Nelly. The woman was a mystery.

"Ned," he muttered. "There's a stagehand named Ned, isn't there?"

"And two Edward's. One's an actor, the other works in costuming, and as an usher." And what was the bet that the flowers Miss Radcliffe had seen that day, had been sent from a 'Ned'?

Garrett graced her with a smile. "Excellent. Time to go question some Ned's then."

~

THE FIRST NED was a handsome young usher who lifted his

brows incredulously when they asked him if there had been any sort of relationship between he and Nelly.

"Me and Nelly Tate?" He repeated, a flush of heat burning into his cheeks. "Cor, if I 'ad been seein' 'er, you'd 'ave known it. I'd be shoutin' that from the rooftops. Blimey, to 'ave 'alf the luck!" Then his delight faded. "Or mebbe not. Lord Rommell wouldn't 'ave cared much for that."

"It's definitely not him," Garrett muttered under his breath as they went in search of Ned the stagehand. "I'm fairly certain he wouldn't be able to pen such an eloquent play."

"Interesting how he seemed afraid of Rommell," Perry replied quietly.

Their eyes met in silent understanding and he ushered her through the door to backstage, his hand firm on the small of her back.

A couple of young men were working on shifting some of the props. Two of them were laughing, but the third just looked exhausted, dark circles shadowing his eyes, and his cheeks sunken with gauntness.

The second Perry saw him, she hesitated. "That man asked me if there'd been any news on Nelly the other day. I didn't think anything of it."

Garrett reassessed the fellow. He was tall and lean, with gingery hair. Hardly the sort of chap to steal a young actress of Nelly's caliber, but then one never did know when it came to women.

"Edward Barham?" Garrett called, reviewing the list of names that Fotherham had given him.

The weary-looking fellow looked up. The second he saw them, he paled, then turned and bolted through the door.

"It's him!" Perry snapped, after a shocked moment of hesitation.

They thundered after him.

Barham led them a merry chase through the wings, and across the stage. He leapt down into the orchestra pit, and scrambled up into the seating.

Perry followed, the long flap of her leather jacket flaring out around her like wings as she leapt. Garrett made as if to follow but something caught his eye; a shadow moving above, in the flies.

What the–?

He saw the glint of light reflect back off metal, and realization dealt him a swift blow to the gut.

"Look out!" he roared, leaping off the stage, and going after her.

Perry's feet skidded to a halt, and she glanced over her shoulder at him. It was the only thing that saved her life.

A shot rang out, sparks ringing off the metal ladder nearby. It missed Perry by an inch. Garrett slammed into her, carrying her to the floor, and rolling his body between them. The world faded to red as the hunger roared through his veins, fury bringing with it a wave of murderous intent. His sight grew clearer, the world snapping into sharp relief as the predator within him roused.

"Son of a bitch!" Perry looked up in shock toward the flies, "Did someone just–"

Yes. His blood ran cold. "Stay down."

Garrett rolled her out of the way, shoving her behind a seat. He drew his own pistol, looking up. The shadow moved, running along the metal frame. "Looks like my ploy worked." He just hadn't expected an attempt to be made against Perry, and that pissed him off. He should have.

Perry craned her neck, focusing on the door that was still flapping from Ned Barham's exit. "Bloody hell."

"Go." He gave her a shove. "Hunt Barham down. I'll take care of this." It was the safest option.

"No!" Her eyes blazed, and he knew she was thinking about what had happened the last time they'd separated.

"I'm not going to get shot." Garrett could just make out the edge of the shadow, vanishing into the darkness of the wings. He needed to move and now, if he wanted any chance at catching the bastard. "We need to know why Barham's running," he reminded her. "We need to confirm our suspicions about Nelly and Hobbs."

Perry wavered. She slid her aural communicator into her ear and hooked it there, "Keep in contact with me." Both wrist-pistols slipped into her palms, and her fingers clenched around them. "And watch your back. I'll be there as soon as I can."

"Always." Garrett's gaze returned to the wings, tracking their assailant, and he darted forward, using the edge of the stage to cover himself.

NED BARHAM HAD a good start on her, but that didn't mean much. Perry could pick up hints and traces of his scent as she ran, and it was soon clear that he was using the theatre's secret passages to avoid her. Not running so much now, as gone to ground.

She tracked him to the seamstress' department and entered warily, her double wrist pistols in her hands, just in case someone *else* tried to take a shot at her.

Dust motes circled through the golden patch of sunlight that streamed into the room through the windows. One foot crossing over the other, Perry crept forward, circling a wire fashion mannequin. Racks of clothing provided the perfect hiding place, and she heard a swift intake of breath as she stepped into the patch of sunlight.

"Edward, I have no intention of hurting you. We just wanted to talk about Nelly."

Silence, filled only by two racing heartbeats; hers and one other.

Perry cocked her head. He was in the far corner, behind a row of dresses. Perry held her hands up, flipping her pistols back into their wrist sheaths. Then she held her hands up in the air. "We know you were courting Nelly. We suspect that Nelly is James Hobbs' sister, but we need confirmation of this." She took a step forward. "Edward? Please come out. I know you're there."

No sign of movement, but she heard a muffled sob. Perry stepped forward, and jerked a chartreuse gown out of the way. Edward cowered behind it.

"I didn't do it! I d-didn't do it!" Red seared his pale cheeks, and his eyes were wet with tears. His hands shook as he held them up.

"I know," she said, in a soothing voice. "We know you had nothing to do with Nelly's death. Come out, please."

His breath caught on a sob. Perry stepped closer, sliding one hand over his shaking shoulder, and kneeling as he burst into tears. "Why did you run?"

He shook his head, trying to reign his emotions in. "I don't... k-know... I just saw y-you and ran. I didn't know w-what to think, w-what to do... She's gone." He looked up, face stained with agony. "She's truly gone, and she's n-never coming back, is she?"

"I'm afraid so." Perry's whisper roughened. "The funeral arrangements are being made for this week."

At that Edward burst into a fresh round of sobbing. Perry patted him awkwardly on the shoulder. "I'm sorry to ask this of you, but we truly do need to know what happened. I want to catch whoever did this, and make him pay his dues. Were you courting Nelly in secret? Did her brother not approve?"

The whole story spilled out in bits and pieces; Edward - or Ned's - shy friendship with the young actress, slowly turning to something more. He'd never expected Nelly to ever return his feelings, and they often walked in the park before rehearsal to get away from the mayhem of the theatre. Nelly had begun to confide in him about her difficult upbringing with a mother who didn't approve of her desires for a theatre life. The young Eleanor Hobbs had run away to London to join the theatre, and her older half-brother James, who she knew little of.

"James encouraged her to take another name to protect his business, when it became apparent she intended to be an actress - with or without his help. James adored her, but he made his feelings on her lifestyle clear. He wanted her to marry and settle down - just not with me." Ned's eyes were glazed with exhaustion, his tears drying and chapping his cheeks. "He knew I belonged in the theatre, and he wanted to remove her from its temptations. And then, of course, there was Rommell, and Beckham, and a half dozen others who thought they could buy her... So we kept our... our engagement a secret."

"You were engaged?"

Ned nodded miserably, and reached inside his collar to withdraw a small golden band on a strip of leather around his throat. "I was keeping it safe for her, for when we could finally announce our intentions to the world. I don't know what I'm going to do," he whispered, his heart breaking in his eyes. "Nelly believed in me. She believed that I could do anything, that I could become more than... than just a stage-hand. I loved her so much."

The poor bastard. She had to get going - Garrett was alone with a murderer -but sympathy kept her there for a few moments longer... "Then do what she wanted you to do. Publish the play. It's quite good, actually. I read the little notes she'd been making - that's how we knew to track you down."

Ned stared at her blankly, then resolve started to come into his eyes. "She'd have wanted that."

Perry straightened, and helped drag Ned to his feet. "Do you have any idea who might have wished her ill?"

That changed his demeanour. "It's the only reason I've been able to come back to work," he confessed. "I keep thinking maybe I'll see or hear something. Maybe I could find them."

"You don't think the clockwork menace had anything to do with it? Everyone else seems to."

"Lovecraft would never have hurt her!" Ned looked up guiltily. "I met him once, see. When James first threw me out of his shop – and Nelly often spoke of him."

"Lovecraft?" she suggested, to keep him focused.

"He adored Nelly. She was his 'aunt'. The poor blighter wouldn't have hurt a fly, and definitely not Nelly. James took him in, but Nelly... She always made an effort to look out for the less fortunate, you know? She made him feel like he belonged, like there was nothing wrong with him."

"I'm so sorry," Perry said again, uselessly.

Ned looked like he'd been disemboweled by grief. There was as much life left in him as the fashion mannequin.

"I have to go," she said. The tick of time seemed to fire blood through her veins. Where was Garrett? Was he all right? Had she taken too long? But first– "I promise you that we shall do everything in our power to bring whoever did this to justice."

It wasn't much, not with Ned's entire life torn apart. But it was the only thing she could offer him.

A bark of sound echoed in the distance, so quietly that she almost missed it. Perry cocked her head, and cut Ned off as he opened his mouth to say something. A second echo followed. The moment she recognised it, she had no thought left for either Ned or Nelly.

That had sounded like pistol fire.

15

G arrett pounded through the backstage, following the shadowy figure ahead. It was a circular chase, almost as though the bastard was leading him somewhere. He crashed through a door and–

Something moved in the corner of his vision.

A weapon discharged with a flash of light, and the second before the bullet hit him, he had the thought - *bloody hell, there are two of them*–

Heat and fire slammed into Garrett's shoulder. It felt like a punch and he staggered back into the wall, the scent of blood igniting all of the darker urges within him. The room swam, full of shadows as he tried to get his feet underneath him.

A trap. A bloody trap.

He had to get out of here. Clapping a hand to his shoulder, Garrett forced his suddenly-heavy legs to drive him behind a prop. Another bullet bit into the wall where he'd been standing, and a cold sweat sprang up along his spine. Someone was trying to kill him, and if he didn't pull himself together, they'd succeed.

Where was Perry? Why the hell had he sent her away? Stubborn, bloody pride, that was why, driving him to protect her. Now he was the one who needed help.

Would she even hear the shot?

His right leg gave out, and Garrett went down to his knee, pain tearing through his shoulder, and his pistol skittering from nerveless fingers. His vision blurred. The pistol came to a halt several feet away.

How badly was he bleeding? Through the shadowed haze that filled his vision, he could just make out his right hand, slippery with darkened blood. His blood.

Footsteps stalked him. Garrett clenched his teeth together, and dived for the pistol.

"There he is!" Someone barked.

Even through the ringing of his ears, the man's tone was crisp and precise. Garrett had spent years mimicking a man's proper speech, and trying to erase all hints of his own roughened Bethnal accent. He knew what that sounded like.

The Echelon.

Rommell.

Then who the hell had originally shot at them in the flies?

Using another prop as cover, Garrett tried to steady his shaking hand. His wet fingers were slippery on the trigger. Where was the first assailant? He ducked his head around the prop, trying to see the pair of them, and another shot rang out, spraying shards of brick over him as it hit the wall.

Pinned down. Garrett swore under his breath. All they'd have to do is flank him, and he was done for.

Touching the brass aural communicator in his ear, he pressed the button to connect it. "Perry?"

A moment of static, and then, "Where the hell are you?"

"Backstage. There are two of them. They've got me

trapped." His vision blurred for a second, and Garrett swallowed hard.

"I'm coming," she snapped, the communicator turning her voice tinny. "Just hold on, princess, and I shall rescue you."

Garrett tipped his head back and let out a shaky laugh. She'd gotten him out of stickier situations than this in the past. He just hoped she made it in time.

Priming the pistol, Garrett ducked around the prop, and aimed a shot off, nearly hitting Rommell. His lordship ducked with a startled curse, as though he couldn't believe anyone would dare try and shoot him. Garrett slammed back behind the prop, and tipped his head back, breathing hard. He had five shots remaining. Just enough to hopefully keep them at bay, and give Perry time to get there.

"So, it *was* you, Rommell," Garrett called. "What happened? Finally grew weary of being rebuffed by a theatre actress? It seems not even you can buy everything you want."

"That bitch should have known where her loyalties lay," Rommell snapped. "I'm not the type of man one mocks."

"So you killed her?"

"As if I got my own hands dirty," Rommell snarled.

That explained his alibi for the day Nelly went missing. He'd bloody paid someone else to do the job.

The other assailant, no doubt.

"How did you find out that Nelly's heart lay elsewhere?" Thoughts raced through Garrett's mind. Was it the posy of peonies that had tipped Rommell off? "You had someone in the theatre spying on her, didn't you?" If so, then Rommell had put someone into the theatre only recently - as the first lot of peonies had come on Nelly's birthday - and from the theatre records, only one man had been recently employed.

"It's Millington, isn't it? You saw the peonies, and how much Nelly adored them, and so you set someone into the theatre to find out who had sent her the flowers. And he tracked Nelly back to James Hobb, didn't he?" No doubt Nelly had gone to visit her brother, never knowing just what trouble was following her.

"Very well done, Reed," Rommell's voice was silky. "A shame you're not going to be able to do anything about this information."

"Lovecraft saw Hobbs die, and followed Millington back to the theatre, didn't he?" Garrett continued, as though he'd said nothing.

"Actually, I walked straight into him as I were leavin' Hobbs' shop," Millington offered. "Guess the filthy bastard figured out what had happened, and followed me."

"I'm here," Perry whispered, through the aural communicator. *"Keep them talking. I'm going after Millington. His lordship's holding that pistol like it's a dueling weapon, but Millington's creeping up on your left."*

Relief was swift. "Be careful," he whispered, then lifted his head to call, "A shame that Millington wasn't more thorough. You killed the wrong man. Hobbs was Nelly's half-brother. Her lover is still alive."

Silence greeted his response.

"What?" Rommell asked, in the kind of voice that indicated he had directed his words at Millington.

"Don't move!" Perry's voice rang out from behind them all. "You're both under arrest for murder, and conspiracy to murder."

A shot rang out, and Perry cursed. Three more shots fired in rapid succession.

That drove Garrett to his feet. "Perry?" he called, easing past the prop just enough to see. Was she all right?

Millington was dead on the ground at Perry's feet, and she had her pistol trained on Rommell, who returned the stance.

Garrett eyed his lordship through his own shaking sights. "Drop your weapon, my lord. I won't hesitate in shooting you." A nasty little smile curled over his mouth. "Indeed, I'd quite enjoy it."

Rommell stepped forward coldly, his pistol focused on Perry, and his eyes flickering to Garrett. "And now we face a conundrum, Reed. Because I'll shoot the bitch, regardless of whether I go down too. I promise you that. Perhaps you should put your we–"

Perry kicked the pistol out of Rommell's hand. She spun, drilling her knee up into Rommell's balls, and then drove an elbow sideways into his ear when he crumpled with a scream.

"You, my lord, are under arrest," she said, yanking the pair of manacles from her belt, and jerking Rommell's arms up behind him with visible relish. She snapped the cuffs into place. "For orchestrating the murders of Nelly Tate, James Hobbs, and the man known as Lovecraft."

"One crucial mistake, my lord." Garrett gave a pained laugh. "You should never underestimate a woman with a gun."

Rommell looked like he was crying. "You b-bitch! Don't you know who... I am...?"

Perry stuffed her handkerchief in his lordship's mouth, and gagged him. "Of course I know who you are. You're the man who's going to be decapitated for his crimes. It's going to be all through the papers, so all of London society shall know who you are too."

"Nice work," Garrett said, leaning back against the wall, and pressing his hand against the bullet wound in his shoulder. Pain flared up his nerves, but he breathed through it.

"I just needed his attention focused elsewhere." Perry gave a fluid shrug. "Thank you." Then her eyes locked on him, her irises darkening as the hunger within her rose. "You're bleeding."

"I'll live." Garrett slid down the wall, his back pressed hard against the timber paneling. Bloody hell. His legs felt like jellied meat.

Stepping over Rommell, Perry hurried to Garrett's side and knelt, the tight leather of her trousers straining over her lean thighs. "Are you all right?"

"Rommell's about as good a shot as he is at seducing women."

"Bad jests? I guess you can't be that injured." Still, she frowned. "Let me look at it."

Garrett endured her poking and prodding. Her dark hair tumbled over her eyes as she bent her head closer to examine his wound. "Through and through," she said, in relief. "By the time we get back to the Guild, it probably won't even require stitching. It's already healing."

"Excellent." He felt somewhat dizzy; just enough that he actually leaned toward her.

Perry slipped her shoulder under his. Vanilla oil flavoured the air he breathed, along with the faint scent of the soap she used. "Do you think you're well enough to stand? I'll need to contact the Guild so that they may fetch Rommell."

The faint flicker of her pulse in her throat caught Garrett's attention. His vision blackened out again, becoming nothing more than shadows as the hunger surged within him.

Garrett squeezed his eyes shut and swallowed. "Perry," he warned.

She knew better than to come near an injured blue-blood. Stillness radiated through her as Perry realized it. Feeling her gaze upon him, he opened his own eyes.

Hers were very big and gray, surrounded by thick dark lashes. She was so close, that if he wasn't reigning himself in sharply, Garrett could have closed his fist in her hair, and dragged her head back to reveal that tantalizing throat.

And she knew it too. Perry's startled outtake of breath dampened his lips. Her eyes widened even further, and for a moment he was lost in them, as blackness chased the color from her irises.

So close... And he wanted to do it, Garrett realized. Wanted to taste the sweet, cool slide of her blood. Every muscle in his core trembled from the sheer *want* of it. *Hell.* He turned his face away, letting out a shuddering breath.

"Here." Perry tugged a flask of blood from inside her coat, and unscrewed the lid, her cheeks flushing with color. "Drink this."

He could almost scent the heated blood in her veins, and his darkened gaze dipped to her throat once more, but Garrett forced himself to drink from the flask, sating some part of his dark hungers, at least.

A bloodletting was always an intimate event between a blue blood, and the woman he drank from. It was also highly pleasurable for both of them. His cock hardened at the thought, and Garrett shifted his knee so that Perry wouldn't notice.

Hell, if she even suspected where his thoughts were going she'd probably drive a knee into said balls. She'd never let him forget it either. Or no, he thought, glancing at the color in her cheeks - perhaps she would. Perhaps they'd both pretend it had never happened.

It's not *going to happen. Not her*, he told himself angrily - or the darker, hungrier part that didn't care that she was his friend and partner.

The hunger. That was all this was. Though he'd never felt its grip quite this tightly before.

You've never been shot before, either, he reminded himself.

"Thanks." Garrett handed her the flask, and tipped his head back in a sigh. The burning sensation in his shoulder had lessened, and the room wasn't swimming as much as it had been.

"Think you can manage?" she asked.

"I'm fine. I'll keep an eye on Rommell."

"Good." Perry straightened. "I'll go send a 'gram to the Guild."

Garrett watched her go, and breathed a little sigh of relief that she was no longer here to torment him.

16

L ynch leaned back in his chair, his fingers forming a steeple in his lap as he listened to their report. "The one thing I don't understand is how Rommell thought he would get away with murdering two Nighthawks, let alone three other people?"

"It's a particular failing of his," Garrett replied diplomatically. "Rommell seems to think he can buy his way out of any problem."

"His head is in his arse, sir," Perry added.

Lynch's firm mouth softened into a faint smile as he eyed them both. "Is that everything?"

"Yes, sir," Garrett said, standing to attention. "Though Rommell's demanding a trial before the Council of Dukes. Says no human murder is going to bring down a man of his standing, and that he didn't get his hands dirty - that Millington planned it all."

Lynch grimaced. "That's going to be hard to prove."

"Not impossible. We have bank records for Millington, proving a rather substantial sum was deposited there by Lord Rommell, plus Rommell's stated confession to both

Perry and I. And the murder weapon was discovered to have come from Rommell's collection - he's a weapons enthusiast, though he has more skill at collecting them, than using them. Both the Webley and the Colt are accounted for, according to his records, and Fitz is adamant that they were used in the murders."

Lynch slowly nodded. "Good work. I'll see if I can place some pressure on the Council to make the right choices. An example should be made. If the human classes realize that the Echelon is trying to hush this up, they'll end up rioting."

"Thank you, sir," both Perry and Garrett echoed.

The chair creaked as Lynch leaned back in it. "And your argument? You've worked matters out between you?"

Without looking, Garrett knew Perry was blushing. "We have," he told Lynch. "A minor disagreement, nothing else. It's done."

Or at least, he hoped it was bloody well done.

"This doesn't happen again, do you both understand?" Lynch's eyes were lazy and hooded, but Garrett knew that it didn't make the guild master any less dangerous.

"It won't happen again," Perry said. The vehemence in her voice made him look at her.

"It won't happen again," Garrett agreed, in a quieter voice, though he was thinking of what had almost happened to her, rather than the argument.

That was over now. He had to keep telling himself that. Perry was safe, and now that she'd accepted the knife from him, he'd always have a way to find her if he needed to. The tracking device was a small, hard lump in his coat pocket, correlating directly to the beacon in the knife.

A crisp nod - the matter was evidently finished in Lynch's eyes. "Dismissed, then."

They both let out a sigh of relief.

~

Two days later...

THE TEAHOUSE near the Guild was filled with the noise of teacups rattling against their saucers, and the dull murmur of conversation. Perry sank back into a studded, red leather armchair, and shook out the paper.

Garrett leaned on the edge of her chair, and peered over her shoulder, tugging at the top page. "Not even the bloody front page. How's that for gratitude?"

"Lynch is trying to keep Rommell's part in this quiet until the court case is finalized," she said irritably, shaking the paper free of his grasp, and smoothing the crumpled sheets. "His house is a powerful one. The Duke of Morioch is his cousin, I believe."

"Don't know how you keep track of them all..." His voice trailed off, which was good, as she didn't quite know how to answer that.

Lie to him about her origins? The thought made her feel uncomfortable. They rarely spoke about where they'd come from, and she was quite content with that. After all, what was she to say? *Surprise, Garrett, I grew up with a copy of Lady Hammersley's Guide to the Peerage in my hands. I know every lord in the land, and even their consorts and thralls - or I did once. I also know how to curtsy and dance, and play the pianoforte horrendously...*

And I'm not quite as innocent as you presume.

After all, Perry knew what had put *that* look into his eyes that day in the theatre, when he'd been shot. The craving. It wasn't the first time that a man had looked at her like that. She knew what it felt like for a man's weight to press down over hers, his lips to brush against her throat, his blood-letting knife finding purchase there with a sharp sting...

Perry suppressed a shudder of mingled lust and fear. *The duke will never find you. You know that. And you're a blue blood now, not a frightened young thrall, with no allies, no one to turn to...*

That girl is dead. You buried her - and the past - and no one is ever going to find out she still exists.

A part of her wished she believed the words she told herself.

The sound of heeled boots on the timber floorboards caught her attention. That, and the sudden stiffening through Garrett's hard frame. Perry looked up, pushing away thoughts of the past.

Miss Radcliffe swirled her parasol on the floor, her lacy gloves tightening over her knuckles. She smiled hesitantly, dark eyes flashing over the pair of them. "I apologise for the interruption. I called at the Guild, but your friend, Mr Byrnes, gave me your direction here."

She wasn't speaking to Perry. Perry tried to sink into the armchair, but there was nowhere for her to go. She had a great deal of respect for the young lady. Miss Radcliffe had shown incredible grace during a difficult time; what with Nelly's murder, the pressure of stepping into the lead role, and Rommell using Millington to try and scare Miss Radcliffe into his bed, with his fake-kidnapping attempt in the back alley, and the red roses from a 'mysterious suitor'. That didn't mean that Perry wanted to witness this conversation.

Garrett straightened. "Miss Radcliffe, you're doing well?"

Perry dragged the newspaper up in front of her face, in lieu of escaping.

"I-I hope you don't think me forward." Miss Radcliffe

sounded breathy. "I thought perhaps you might care to... to take a stroll in the park? Or perhaps that play we spoke of?"

Every muscle in her body locked up tight, and Perry flipped the page, trying to focus. She'd made a promise to herself to guard her emotions better. It was harder to keep than she'd expected.

Garrett hesitated, then let his weight sink back onto the edge of the seat. "Some other time, perhaps."

It was a clear dismissal. Perry shot Miss Radcliffe a shocked glance, then looked away swiftly, knowing that guilt drove him. Miss Radcliffe would never grace Garrett's bed, because he'd never be able to look at her without thinking of Perry's near-drowning.

Perry tried not to listen as Miss Radcliffe stammered her goodbyes. It didn't matter if he said no this time. There'd always be another Miss Radcliffe. Another blonde, or brunette, or redhead, but it wouldn't matter, because it would never be a young woman with dyed black hair, and the harsh black leather body armour of a Nighthawk.

It would never be *her*.

"What's wrong?"

Perry looked up, hot blue eyes meeting hers. There was nothing of guile about his gaze. Perhaps that was what she admired most about Garrett. What you saw was what you got. He truly cared for people, and was astonishingly perceptive toward their moods. Particularly hers. "Nothing," she lied and tried to paste a smile on her lips. "You should go after Miss Radcliffe," she made herself say. "The case is over and she... she has my approval. She's much nicer than your usual standard of conquest."

"Is she now?" He grimaced. "No. I don't think I will."

"You deserve to take some time off after such a case. A walk in the park would do you good."

"No, Perry." His expression twisted. "My heart's not in it. Besides, I had something else in mind." Reaching inside his jacket, he produced a pair of tickets. "'*A Lady Well Educated.*' It's playing at the Royalty this evening. Not quite the tragedy you prefer, but I'm told it's hilarious. Somewhat risqué perhaps." His shoulder nudged hers, his gaze a challenge. "You might enjoy it. Care to join me?"

Perry stared at the tickets, her heart starting a slow kick in her chest. *It means nothing.* And perhaps it would be good to do something together. Something that would reaffirm their friendship, and place this whole mess in the past.

A truce.

"I'd much rather see something like a '*A Gentleman Well Behaved*'," she drawled, "but why not?"

"A well-behaved gentleman is a rather boring affair." He caught her fingers and dragged her to her feet, the paper tumbling to the floor. "And good, for they cost me a small fortune. Best seats in the house... and I don't just do that for anyone, luv."

His wicked smile turned her heart, but Perry ruthlessly fought it down. It was past time to put aside her hurt feelings - and these newer, troubling ones that afflicted her. Time to bury them for good, for nothing could ever come of them.

"Aren't I special then?" she said, and knew the words meant nothing.

∾

BEFORE YOU LEAVE THE LONDON STEAMPUNK
WORLD

Dear Reader,

Thanks for reading *The Clockwork Menace*. I hope you enjoyed it! Want to know what happens when Perry finally reveals her hand? Enjoy their romance in *Forged By Desire*.

If you want more fantasy-fuelled romance, I recommend starting my London Steampunk: The Blue Blood Conspiracy series.

Mission: Improper kicks off with Caleb Byrnes encountering an old flame from his past....

Available now:

Mission: Improper
The Mech Who Loved Me
You Only Love Twice
To Catch A Rogue
Dukes Are Forever

Want to know more about future release dates?

Make sure you sign up to my newsletter to be the first to know when they're available.

Here are some other ways to stay updated:

* Follow me on Bookbub
* Visit my website at becmcmaster.com
*Or join my Facebook Fan Group for all the exclusive stuff!

I hope we meet again between the pages of another book!

Cheers,
Bec McMaster

*P.S Not ready to leave London? Read on for a preview of what's next for Byrnes and a mysterious femme fatale in **Mission: Improper**...*

READ NOW

Entire families have gone missing in the East End.

When Caleb Byrnes receives an invitation to join the Company of Rogues as an undercover agent pledged to protect the crown, he jumps at the chance to find out who, or what, is behind the disappearances. Hunting criminals is what the darkly driven blue blood does best, and though he prefers to work alone, the opportunity is too good to resist.

The problem?

He's partnered with Ingrid Miller, the fiery and passionate verwulfen woman who won a private bet against him a year ago. Byrnes has a score to settle, but one stolen kiss and suddenly the killer is not the only thing Byrnes is interested in hunting.

Soon they're chasing whispered rumours of a secret project gone wrong, and a monster that just might be more dangerous than either of them combined.

The only way to find out more is to go undercover among the blue blood elite...

EXCERPT

"Miss you?" Byrnes stated flatly, though the gleam in his blue eyes wasn't cold.

Not at all.

He took a menacing step toward her before pausing, his lean form falling into absolute stillness.

Ingrid Miller smiled. She'd worked with Byrnes for only two weeks—or worked against him, perhaps, when he'd declared that he didn't need her and could find the suspect before she could—but in that time she'd come to know him well enough to predict him.

He hated emotional displays, especially in himself. His control was absolute. And she'd just caused him to break both of those self-governed rules.

Call it the devil on her shoulder, but when it came to Byrnes, she absolutely could not help herself.

"Miss you?" he repeated. "Why yes... I believe I did. I have a little debt to repay."

"A *little* debt?" Ingrid glanced at him from beneath her lashes in a most un-Ingrid-like way. "What a curious choice of words."

Instantly his gaze flattened, and she laughed.

"I searched for you," he said stiffly.

"Did you?"

"I spent months looking for you."

"You wouldn't have found me, no matter how much time you spent looking for me."

You wouldn't have found me, because I wasn't here.

"Where did you go after the Drury Lane case? You weren't in London. You weren't in any of the towns nearby. You weren't even in bloody Scotland!"

"That's not really any of your business."

"Oh, I think it is." Byrnes was in her space. They were of a height, especially with her in her heeled boots, but she never felt unfeminine around him, the way she sometimes felt with other men. Byrnes always challenged her to be an equal, and that look in his eye had always made her feel distinctly feminine.

"You left me naked and bound to my bed. I've been thinking about what I'd do to you to repay the debt for the last year." His voice dropped. "Oh, and Ingrid, I've had time to get very creative about it."

"Poor Caleb. It sounds like I got to you."

He *hated* it when she called him Caleb.

His teeth ground together, and he reached out to cup her cheek. One thumb brushed against her cheek, then lower, to her mouth, sinking into her plush lower lip and pressing just firmly enough to rouse a fire in her blood. Byrnes leaned closer. "That happens when a woman makes certain promises, and then reneges upon them."

"I promised to get you naked," she whispered around the press of his thumb. "You were naked, if I recall. We never agreed upon anything else."

"You wrote on me."

"It was a lovely little poem. 'There was a young Nighthawk from Matlock; Who had a fairly significant—"

"I remember," he growled under his breath, blue eyes lighting with fury and desire.

"I'm sure you do."

I am going to repay this debt tenfold, his eyes seemed to say.

You can certainly try, replied her smile.

That made his eyes narrow.

"Miss me, Byrnes?" she murmured, her voice dropping to a whisper as her body softened toward his. The devil always had this effect upon her. "It certainly sounds like it."

"Only because I mean revenge, Miller."

Miller. God knew she'd missed that, strangely enough. Ingrid's smile softened and she bit the thumb that still lingered on her lip. The heat in his gaze turned intense, and he sucked in a sharp breath.

"Admit it," she said, sucking his thumb gently. "It was more than revenge."

CONTINUE READING

ALSO BY BEC MCMASTER

DARK COURT RISING

A new fantasy series with a fairytale twist, inspired by the Hades and Persephone myth.

Promise of Darkness

(coming September 2019)

LONDON STEAMPUNK SERIES

Kiss Of Steel

Heart Of Iron

My Lady Quicksilver

Forged By Desire

Of Silk And Steam

Novellas in same series:

Tarnished Knight

The Clockwork Menace

LONDON STEAMPUNK: THE BLUE BLOOD CONSPIRACY

Mission: Improper

The Mech Who Loved Me

You Only Love Twice

To Catch A Rogue

Dukes Are Forever

DARK ARTS SERIES

Shadowbound

Hexbound

Soulbound

BURNED LANDS SERIES

Nobody's Hero

The Last True Hero

The Hero Within

LEGENDS OF THE STORM SERIES

Heart Of Fire

Storm of Desire

Clash of Storms

Storm of Fury (coming 2019)

SHORT STORIES

The Many Lives Of Hadley Monroe

Burn Bright

ABOUT THE AUTHOR

BEC MCMASTER is a writer, a dreamer, and a travel addict.
If she's not sitting in front of the computer, she's probably
plotting her next overseas trip, and hopes to see the whole
world, whether it's by paper, plane, or imagination.

Bec grew up on a steady diet of '80s fantasy movies like
Ladyhawke, *Labyrinth*, and *The Princess Bride*, and loves
creating epic, fantasy-based romances with heroes and
heroines who must defeat all the odds to have their HEA.
She lives in Australia with her very own hero, where she can
be found creating the worlds of the London Steampunk,
Dark Arts, Legends of The Storm, or Burned Lands series,
where even the darkest hero can find love.

Read more at <u>www.becmcmaster.com</u>
THE END

Made in the USA
Coppell, TX
25 September 2020

38693570R10100

OCT 23 2020